Haunted Inheritance

Haunted

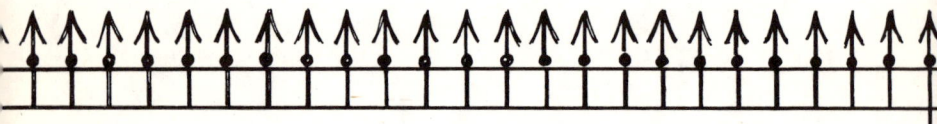

Published by

Minneapolis, Minnesota
A division of Comprehensive Care Corporation

(Ask for our catalog, 800/328-3330, toll free outside Minnesota
or 612/559-4800, Minnesota residents)

Inheritance

LUCY BARRY ROBE

Illustrations by Mimi Noland

ST. PHILIP'S COLLEGE LIBRARY

© 1980 by Lucy Barry Robe

All rights reserved.
Published in the United States
by CompCare Publications.

Library of Congress Catalog Card No. 79-56803
ISBN 0-89638-042-4

Reproduction in whole or part, in any form, including storage in memory device system, is forbidden without written permission . . . except that portions may be used in broadcast or printed commentary or review when attributed fully to author and publication by names.

All of the characters in this book are fictitious, and any resemblance to actual persons, living or dead, is purely coincidental.

Other books by Lucy Barry Robe

Just So It's Healthy (CompCare Publications)
Stagestruck Secretary (William Morrow and Company)

*For my beloved daughter, Parrish,
who learned to read as this was
being written.*

The Lyon Family

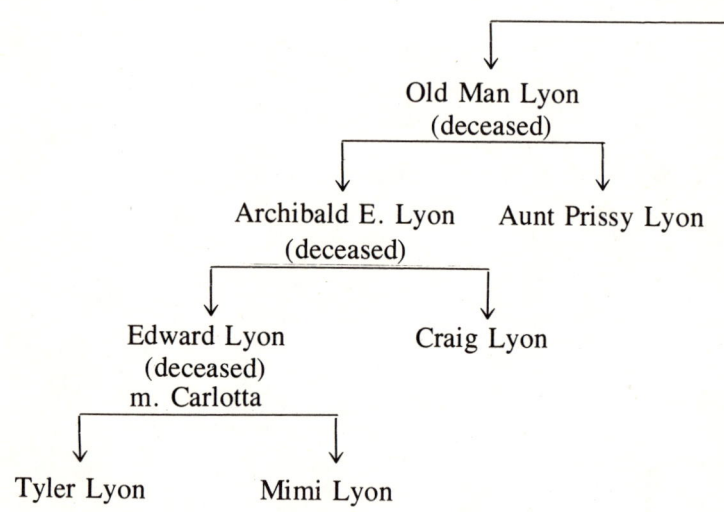

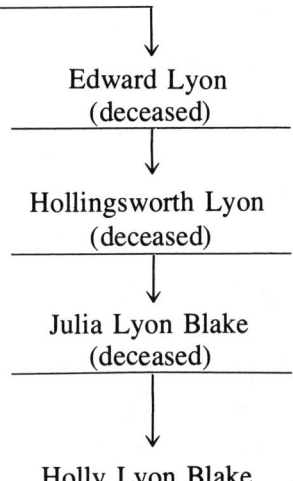

Edward Lyon
(deceased)

Hollingsworth Lyon
(deceased)

Julia Lyon Blake
(deceased)

Holly Lyon Blake

Chapter 1

Holly had fantasized sometimes about what it would be like to turn up in some distant relative's will. Now—through a twist of fortune—that was actually happening. Would her inheritance be just an old cameo brooch, she wondered aloud, or enough money so she would be able to quit her part-time campus job next fall?

Her friend Gay guided the car between impressive stone posts topped with carved lions. A discreet brown and gold sign stated: LYON HOUSE—Private Way.

"If this is the place, Hol," said Gay, "you may be in for a whole lot more than a cameo brooch."

The paved driveway wound through a thick forest, emerging a good quarter mile later to a glittering view of Long Island Sound and the distant Connecticut shoreline.

Holly was stunned. Sprawled clear across the crest of a hill, Lyon House was a Tudor-style beige stucco mansion, decorated with wide lattices of brown wooden trim. Five bays protruded at irregular intervals. The steeply pitched grey slate roof was crowned by massive chimneys topped by triple smoke stacks.

"You never told me your mother's folks were loaded," said Gay.

"I had no idea," Holly said, giddily comparing this spread with her own modest home.

"How come?"

Holly shrugged uncomfortably. "Family feud." Her parents had died suddenly here on Long Island when she was only six. She had been brought up in Vermont by her paternal grandparents, who loathed her mother's family.

"I've never met the Lyons," she said. "I didn't even know about Archibald Lyon's death until the funeral was over. What'll I do if they put me down?"

1

"Don't take it personally," said Gay bluntly. "They can't toss you out, even if they want to. You were invited by their lawyer."

Nervously, Holly pressed the ornate brass bell. The front door was opened by a Japanese man, dressed in black trousers and a starched white mess jacket.

"I'm Holly Blake. Mr. Dodd asked me to be here at four o'clock." Having no experience with butlers, Holly didn't know whether or not to identify Gay.

The man said impassively, "This way, please," and on black slippered feet he led them into an immense entrance hall.

A giant elliptical arch framed a broad staircase. The paneled walls were lined with Elizabethan furniture, paintings, and artifacts. A foot-high statue of a pair of hands on the newel post glowed eerily in the sharp beam of a spotlight.

The house was absolutely silent. "Is anybody else here?" Holly inquired shyly.

"You wait." The houseman motioned the girls into a library. "They come four o'clock," he said and left.

"Will you look at all those books!" Gay gestured at floor-to-ceiling bookcases on three walls of the room.

The fourth wall featured a giant stone fireplace, over which hung a portrait of a fiercely-moustached, white-haired man wearing a nautical uniform. The artist had managed somehow to make his subject's stern brown eyes stare directly at the viewer from any position in the room. Holly gazed intently at it, hoping to trigger a memory of her mother, but with no success.

"Who's the old relic?" Gay asked. "He looks almost alive."

"Probably Archibald Lyon himself," Holly said.

"Hi, girls." A good-looking blond man about their age strolled into the room. "Who're you?" he asked Gay.

"I'm Gay Thayer and this is—"

"Are you related to Cadwallader Thayer of Philadelphia?" the boy interrupted her in a preppy, hot-potato accent. "Caddy was in my class at Groton. He had red hair, too."

"I think he's a distant cousin," Gay drawled in return.

Holly restrained a grin. She knew Gay had no fancy relatives.

The young man turned to Holly. "And you are . . . ?"

"Holly Blake."

"So, you're little Cousin Holly!" A stocky old woman wearing running shoes bounced through a French door and plopped herself on a needlepointed window seat. "She's your third cousin, Tyler," she announced. "Your Cousin Julia's daughter. Your grandfather, Holly, was Archibald's and my first cousin—he was our Uncle Edward's boy, Hollingsworth."

"No kidding?" Tyler suddenly seemed less friendly. "Are you a cousin, too, Gay? Caddy never mentioned—"

"No way," said Gay hastily. "I just gave Holly a lift down from Vermont on my way home to New Jersey."

The old lady yanked a piece of needlepoint from a tennis tote. "Relatives have a way of turning up for will readings, 'specially juicy ones." She laughed so heartily that the strands of grey hair straying from her topknot danced.

Holly felt her cheeks turn pink. "I have a telegram from your family lawyer asking me to be here this afternoon," she said.

"Everyone poised for the big moment?" A slim woman in her early forties strode like a panther across the room. "Tyler, dear, I hardly think this is a suitable occasion for guests."

"Aunt Prissy says one of them's a *cousin*, Mother," said Tyler significantly.

The woman's eyes, almond-shaped, and deep green like those of a cat, narrowed at once.

Holly sprang to her feet. "I'm Holly Blake."

"Julia's daughter, Carlotta," said Aunt Prissy.

"You're joking!" Carlotta's voice was shocked. "When did you and Archibald get together?"

"I never met him," Holly told her.

"Then what are you doing here?"

"Mr. Dodd sent me a telegram." Holly dug in her bag for the wire and nodded in Gay's direction. "This is my friend, Gay Thayer."

Carlotta barely acknowledged Gay as she scanned the wire Holly had received yesterday from the family lawyer, informing her of Archibald Lyon's death and inviting her to the will reading.

Rattling china heralded the arrival of the houseman pushing a wagon loaded with silver pots, delicate china, and dainty tea sandwiches. "Over here, Saito." Carlotta's hands trembled as she lifted a cup and saucer. "Who wants tea?"

"How about it, Gay?" Tyler asked. "She's related to Caddy Thayer, Mother."

Carlotta nodded distractedly. "I wonder what *other* surprises Archibald had up his sleeve."

"I think she's a nice surprise," someone said in a deep voice.

Although not handsome in the conventional sense, this young man had crisp dark hair and an aristocratic nose. His eyes were what caught Holly's attention.

"I'm Craig Lyon." He strode over to Holly. "You look familiar. Where have we met?"

"She's Julia's daughter—Holly Blake," said Carlotta tensely.

"So that's it!" Craig grasped Holly's hand. "You have Julia's eyes."

Julia's eyes! Whenever Holly asked her Blake grandparents if she had inherited any of her mother's features, the answer was always a curt: "Julia was too pretty for her own good." Grandpa had destroyed all photographs of Julia the day after her parents died and refused to discuss his daughter-in-law. Time had finally erased Holly's memories until she simply could not remember what her mother looked like.

Until now. For Craig Lyon, she realized, had warm, brown long-lashed eyes *exactly* like her mother's! Frozen in time and space, Holly stared into his eyes as if hypnotized, and Craig looked deeply into hers in return.

Carlotta broke their reverie. "Tea, Craig?"

"I could use something stronger." His voice was hoarse as he pressed Holly's hand, then turned away. "Where's Dad's sherry decanter?"

Saito spoke from the doorway. "Mister Dodd here."

"Where's Mimi?" Carlotta asked him. "Anybody seen Mimi this afternoon? I told that girl to be back by four . . ." Her tone was sharp. "Never mind. Send Mr. Dodd in, Saito. And, Gay, please excuse us. Saito will show you to the drawing room."

Gay winked encouragingly at Holly as she headed out. Then Mr. Dodd came in, fussily dressed for this warm June day in a blue pin-striped business suit.

He was followed by a dark-haired girl about nineteen years old, wearing worn jeans and an oversized T-shirt.

"Where have you been?" Carlotta asked her.

"I'm on time, Mummy," the girl said.

"Mimi, this is your cousin Holly," said Craig.

The girl looked puzzled. "Cousin? Hi, Holly," she added diffidently.

"Holly's been hiding in Vermont all these years. She decided to emerge for the Moment of Truth," Tyler told her.

"Archibald Lyon specifically requested Miss Blake's presence at this meeting," Mr. Dodd told Tyler sharply. "Shall we proceed?" While the attorney opened his briefcase, the others quickly found seats. "This," Mr. Dodd said quietly, "is the last will and testament of Archibald E. Lyon."

Chapter 2

Mr. Dodd stared reverently up at the angry-looking portrait. "I see Mr. Lyon is back in place," he said.

"I found it wrapped in paper in a hall closet," said Aunt Prissy. "Archibald must have sent himself out to be cleaned."

Donning rimless spectacles, Mr. Dodd began to read:

"I, Archibald E. Lyon, being of sound mind and body, do hereby state that only my blood relatives shall participate in my estate."

As someone gasped softly, Holly felt a swift surge of confidence. She *did* belong at Lyon House today!

"Anyone interested in an inheritance must, after hearing this preliminary will, reside at Lyon House for a period of three months."

"No!" cried Mimi in a horrified voice.

Holly was equally stunned. Over Mr. Dodd's balding head, Archibald's wrathful brown eyes challenged her. But, why? After ignoring her all these years?

"The only excuse for non-residency," Mr. Dodd continued reading, "shall be hospitalization."

Holly's mind raced. If she stayed, how would she break the news to Grandpa and Grandma Blake?

"Each family member will contribute a proportionate share to household expenses," droned the lawyer.

"Didn't Archibald leave any *money?*" Carlotta cut in.

"None is stipulated in this document," Mr. Dodd said stiffly. "However, three months' wages have been set aside in escrow for household help."

Saito and a Japanese woman stood just inside the door, faces imperturbable, hands folded on their identical white mess jackets.

"Nothing is to be sold without permission of the trustees,"

Mr. Dodd read on. "Any family member seen intoxicated in a public place by a trustee of the estate will be excluded from any inheritance."

"Who are the trustees?" Craig asked.

"They are anonymous," Mr. Dodd told him, and continued reading. "Behavior of family members should indicate how they would handle my estate. At the end of the three-month period, only family members remaining at Lyon House shall be eligible for inheritance. One will be the sole beneficiary. Signed. . . ." Mr. Dodd concluded, "Archibald E. Lyon."

The library quivered with hushed tension.

"Three months from today will be September first," the lawyer added. "Any questions?" He regarded the stunned group over his rimless spectacles, then handed Holly a creamy envelope festooned with red sealing wax. It was addressed to *Miss Holly Lyon Blake—Personal* in black ink with a firm, old-fashioned hand.

Five pairs of Lyon eyes watched Holly slip the letter into her bag.

"Aren't you going to open it?" Tyler asked.

"That letter is Miss Blake's personal property," Mr. Dodd told him. "These are for you, Craig." He handed the man a stack of airmail envelopes bound with a rubber band. "I'll leave a copy of the will here for reference purposes."

Holly found Gay in a large parlor crowded with Victorian furniture, petting a Siamese cat.

"What did you get?" Gay asked eagerly.

"Nothing yet." Holly sank down on a velvet love seat. "We all have to live here for three months if we want to inherit anything."

"Wow, you mean it's like a contest?"

Holly nodded.

"Boy, do I envy you!" said Gay. "You can swim—learn to sail—there must be tennis courts. A whole summer of nothing to do but vacation!"

"But, Gay—what about the *people?*"

"What about them? Tyler's a bit pompous, but he's really . . . *nice*, you know? And he's been around."

Holly thought fleetingly of Craig, then firmly of the hostility of the others. "I'm not sure I could stand being cooped up with them for three whole months."

"With only thirty or forty rooms, you'll *never* be able to get off by yourself," Gay said drily. "Some torture spending a summer in a mansion, being waited on hand and foot. Did you taste those cucumber-and-watercress sandwiches?"

"I'm supposed to work in Grandpa's drugstore for tuition money," Holly reminded her.

"If you win the jackpot, you'll scribble out a check—like that!" Gay snapped her fingers. "What's the *matter* with you, Holly?"

"I can't figure out why I'm here," Holly said. "We're supposed to show how we'd handle his estate. What do I know about this kind of life?"

Gay looked thoughtful. "Maybe the old boy wanted to put the needle into the others?"

9

"What good would *I* be, a Vermont backwoods hick studying to be a schoolteacher?"

Gay grabbed her by the shoulders. "Holly Blake! Will you quit running yourself down all the time? You're also a *Lyon*, my friend, and *that*'s why you're here!"

"Hi, girls." Tyler spoke from the doorway. "Mother wants to know if you'd like more tea."

"Love some," Gay said quickly.

"I'd like to take a walk," Holly said. "Clear my head a little."

"Try our private beach," Tyler suggested, adding slyly, "you can read Grandfather's letter there in privacy."

A few minutes later, armed with a key from Saito, Holly wandered down the long sloping lawn that fronted the mansion. Rose bushes topped a vertical cliff, bolstered by thick railroad ties, which dropped at least fifty feet to the beach below. To the right, a long flight of wooden steps was blocked halfway down by a small beach house, designed to discourage intruders to the property.

Leaving the key in the lock, Holly propped the door ajar with an iron doorstop, selected a luxurious towel from a neat stack, then strolled down the rest of the steps to the perfect, small sandy beach. The swimming part would be one *good* reason for spending the summer here, she thought, perching cross-legged on her towel facing the harbor.

How often had her mother come to this beach? she wondered, watching seagulls swoop in graceful S-patterns over the water. How frequently had she and Holly's father gone swimming together?

A gull's hoarse cry was her only answer. Waves of regret enveloped Holly for the first time in years; regret that she had lost her parents so young and been deprived by Grandpa Blake of learning anything about her mother.

Until today, when she had come to Lyon House at last, thanks to Archibald Lyon. Holly reached in her bag for his envelope. The stiff, buff-colored sheet of stationery, with LYON HOUSE engraved in gold script, was not dated.

    My dear Holly:
    I have thought a good deal about you recently.

> As you may know, I became your mother's guardian when she was eighteen, after her parents died.

Holly had known that Julia Lyon came East from California at eighteen, married Jack Blake impulsively at nineteen, and died suddenly at twenty-five.

> I was relieved when your grandfather Blake adopted you, because my personal life didn't offer much at that time to a young cousin of six.

Glancing at her opulent surroundings, Holly smiled wryly.

> Also, I had failed tragically in my responsibility to your mother.
>
> So now I can only hope that you won't blame me for your mother's problems, Holly, but will come to realize that she had a disease.

The word "disease" leaped off the page. Did Cousin Archibald mean *mental* disease, Holly wondered with a sinking heart? Was Grandpa right about her mother, after all?

> I know now that it is nothing you need be afraid of inheriting, if you guard closely against it.

Guard against *what*, Holly puzzled? How do you guard against something if you don't know what it is?

> And about your parents' deaths at Lyon House, all I can say is that I am sorry from the bottom of my heart.
>
> For my sake, Holly, will you consider spending this summer at Lyon House? You are, after all, a Lyon—and something very important here is rightfully yours.
>
> There is a clue in the ninth step.
>> Affectionately,
>> Cousin Archibald
>
> P.S. Please keep this letter confidential until the three months are past.

Holly wished that her cousin was still alive. This letter didn't reflect the stern old goat in the library portrait—he sounded very nice! She glanced at the nearby staircase. Could his "ninth step" be right here at the beach?

She was getting up to explore when she heard rustlings above her, followed by a shower of pebbles.

Holly whirled around and saw a large black boulder heading down the cliff. Leaping to one side, she watched the boulder hit the beach, roll directly over her towel, and into the water with a splash.

Holly peered up the cliff. Something white flashed behind a deep yellow rose bush.

"Hey," she shouted, figuring a careless gardener might be at work. "What's going on up there?"

Nobody answered.

Holly took the stairs two at a time to the beach house door, which she found closed and locked. She had left it ajar, she remembered as she rattled the knob. And there was no wind to slam it shut.

Someone had locked the door, returned to the cliff top, and shoved a boulder down at her. Someone wearing white.

Chapter 3

Stooping low, Holly sidled around the beach house and peeked up the cliff. No flash of white behind the roses now. The railway ties reinforcing the cliff were set about eight feet apart. Having hiked regularly in Vermont, she scrambled nimbly up the fifty-foot incline and continued up the steep lawn at a trot. The roofs and chimneys of Lyon House rose menacingly against the sky. Who in that mansion, she wondered, would want to hurt her? Tyler's slacks were white, and Mimi's T-shirt and Aunt Prissy's blouse. And Craig, she recalled unhappily, was wearing a white sports shirt.

Suddenly a white-clad figure rose from behind a nearby bush. Holly screamed as Saito saluted her with a long, gleaming knife.

"Nice sand, miss?" he asked, baring his teeth in a grin. His hands delicately maneuvered the knife among the laurel flowers.

Holly raced on, finally collapsing into a wicker chair on the back terrace.

Carlotta leaned out a window. "What's the matter?" she called.

Holly shook her head, too out of breath to answer, but relieved that Carlotta was wearing gold slacks with a scarlet turtleneck.

The older woman disappeared, then came out carrying a small glass. "Drink this brandy. It'll calm your nerves."

"How long has Saito been at Lyon House?" Holly asked.

Carlotta shrugged. "I don't know. He and Su Chen weren't here two summers ago."

"Did Cousin Archibald trust him?"

Carlotta raised a perfectly arched brow. "I suppose so. He wouldn't have kept Saito otherwise." Her eyes narrowed. "Why do you ask?"

"He sort of . . . surprised me down on the lawn," Holly said lamely.

Carlotta stared out at the harbor. "On the other hand, Archibald *was* unpredictable. He might bequeath the works to the servants—or even to a home for Siamese cats."

"After making us stay here all summer?" Holly cried.

Carlotta shrugged. "You must—we *all* must—consider such a possibility."

Holly gazed down the lawn. The yellow rose bush, alone in a long row of red and pink, seemed to glow mockingly at her in the early evening light.

"Here she is." Gay appeared around a corner with Tyler. "Isn't this place unreal?" Her eyes were shining. "Tyler's been showing me around. He's asked me to stay here for the night."

"The Other Brothers are playing at the Cove Room," Tyler explained to Holly. "I've asked Gay to come along."

Carlotta rose. "I'll have Su Chen show you girls upstairs. Dinner's at seven-thirty, with cocktails first in the drawing room."

Holly's room was appealingly feminine: pink and white flowered wallpaper; white curtains at windows that overlooked Long Island Sound; a needlepoint rug of red, pink, and white roses; a huge canopy bed; and a small fireplace with a white wooden mantel.

She sank into a low rocking chair, thinking of Craig Lyon, whose eyes reminded her so poignantly of her mother. Not surprising, since they had been second cousins. However, she must not forget that Craig could be the boulder-thrower.

"Hey—what a cute room!" Gay burst in without knocking. "It looks as if someone young used to live here. My bathroom has one of those funky toilets with a pull chain. Isn't this some house?"

"Gay," Holly asked thoughtfully, "when Tyler gave you the tour, was he with you the whole time?"

Gay nodded, smiling into the vanity mirror as she fiddled with her hair. Then she added, "Except when he split to make a phone call."

Holly stiffened. "How long did that take?"

"Ten minutes maybe. Why?"

"Well, when I went down to the beach, I sat there thinking about my mother, and—"

"Listen," Gay interrupted her. "Can we talk later? I want to get ready for dinner. What do you think these people will wear?"

Holly glanced at their denim skirts and T-shirts. "Not this."

"I'll lend you a dress," Gay said.

Holly changed into Gay's pretty cotton dress, combed her brown hair loosely over her shoulders, and carefully put on her makeup. Aware that Gay could be a slow dresser, she went downstairs alone. When she entered the drawing room, everyone abruptly stopped talking. She noticed that Aunt Prissy and Mimi wore floor-length skirts and dressy tops and she felt awkward in Gay's simple dress.

The clink of gold bracelets announced Carlotta, who arrived wearing flame silk hostess pajamas. "After the shock of this afternoon, I'm in the mood for a good, strong martini," she announced.

"Coming right up." Craig, elegant in a blazer and light gray slacks, was arranging bottles and glasses on an elaborate bar.

"Your father made a wicked martini, Craig," Carlotta reminisced. "He always boasted they were six to one."

"Try this," Craig said.

"Odd, that clause about not getting inebriated in public," Carlotta remarked. "Remember how he used to love getting a buzz on at parties?"

"He wasn't drinking at all Christmas before last," Aunt Prissy said, her dowdy grey dress enlivened by a quadruple strand of the most enormous yellowed pearls Holly had ever seen.

"Really?" Craig looked interested. "What happened to our traditional Yuletide party with mulled wine?"

"Didn't serve it," said Aunt Prissy. "He had a big group, but most of 'em were strangers."

Craig looked thoughtful. "Maybe Dad's doctors lowered the boom. I can't picture him giving up booze without a medical reason."

"Holly, have you read Grandfather's letter yet?" Tyler asked, as Craig handed her a cocktail.

When she said, "Yes," everyone regarded her with interest.

"What did he say?" Carlotta asked, then added quickly, "Since you're the only one who got a letter from him today, we're *all* curious."

Gazing around at these semi-strangers who were her flesh-and-blood, Holly wished she had their poise and self-confidence. Sharing Cousin Archibald's letter would make them warm up to her, but the old man had specifically asked her not to do it. She took a swallow of her martini, which was so strong she almost choked, but she felt she needed extra courage to say, "It's a beautiful letter, but it's personal."

"Goody gumdrops," Tyler smiled wolfishly. "The old croak was nasty enough to the rest of us. Read us his lovable side, would you?"

"I don't think I should." Holly wished Gay would arrive to lend moral support.

"Oh, come on, Holly. We have a right to know," Tyler persisted, "especially if this competition's going to be a fair one."

"When *I* was a girl, we didn't *dare* conceal matters of import from our elders," said Aunt Prissy loftily.

At that moment, Saito came in with a silver tray of hot hors d'oeuvres. "Is there a gardener here?" Holly asked.

"Dad used a weekly gardening service," Craig told her.

"Did anyone come today?" Holly inquired.

"Why do you ask?" Aunt Prissy nibbled on a bacon-wrapped mushroom.

"I was almost hit by a rock on the beach." Holly chose simple words, hoping Saito would understand. "Someone pushed it down the cliff."

She was sure the houseman turned pale.

Carlotta looked horrified, but Tyler said, "Come off it, Holly. Who would want to harm *you?*"

"Good question," she told him. "I thought it was an accident, but when I went up to check, the beach house door was locked. That's why I didn't bring back the key, Saito."

"Someone passing by probably closed it," Craig said. "Friends often come over by boat to fish."

"There weren't any boats around," said Holly.

"She's inherited her mother's imagination!" Aunt Prissy announced hoarsely, a strange gleam in her eyes. "Remember how Julia used to think people were after her?"

"That boulder came down the cliff directly at me!" Holly

17

protested. "Don't you all realize that I could have been badly hurt? Or even *killed?*"

"Hush, dear." Carlotta spoke soothingly. "Did you see anyone?"

Holly nodded triumphantly. "Someone in white. Hiding behind a yellow rose bush."

Saito glided over to Aunt Prissy, who bent greedily over the hors d'oeuvres again.

"Some*one* or some*thing?*" Tyler asked. "Our beach is crawling with seagulls, Holly."

Holly had not considered that the flash of white behind the rose bush might not be human.

Mimi leaned forward. "Is the rock still on the beach?"

Holly shook her head. "It rolled into the water."

"Vanished evidence," Tyler observed.

"I can show you *exactly* where it went into the harbor!" Holly persisted excitedly, glancing at Craig to gauge his reaction. He was refilling her martini glass and seemed about to speak when Saito offered her his glistening silver platter. Holly shuddered and shook her head, remembering those hands wielding the knife on the lawn. "It wasn't far from the beach house," she said. "We could wade in the water and—"

"Holly, dear, you must calm down," Carlotta cut in briskly. "Meeting the Lyons at long last has been too much excitement for you. As Aunt Prissy says, your mother also had an active imagination. Please, dear, *don't* turn a freak accident into a paranoid fear that someone's out to harm you!" She laughed richly and changed the subject.

Indignantly wondering again if Carlotta was covering up for one of her children, Holly took a swallow of her fresh martini.

"Hi. Sorry I'm late." Gay looked beautiful in an aquamarine skirt with a low-cut dark green top. Her red hair was piled high on her head.

Tyler leaped to his feet. "Have a seat near me. Want a martini?"

They made a dazzling pair, Tyler resplendent in white duck slacks, a navy yachting blazer with a gold club patch, and Gucci loafers.

Settling herself gracefully on a horsehair sofa, Gay took a

dainty sip of her drink, smiled graciously at Tyler, and fell into easy conversation with the Lyons.

Holly was relaxed enough from the martinis to feel confused about the beach incident. Had her imagination run away with her?

Maybe the flash of white *was* just a seagull. And the boulder could have eroded by sheer chance in Holly's direction. After all, she had noticed several other large rocks when she scaled the cliff.

By the time Saito announced dinner, she was almost convinced it had been an accident. Thanks to Gay, she even felt mellower toward the Lyons.

Until Aunt Prissy spoiled it. "I've been looking at your eyes," she told Holly in the dim entrance hall. "They remind me of my aunt's."

"Thank you," Holly said politely.

Aunt Prissy shook her head. "Mad as a hoot owl," she said tapping her forehead with a gnarled finger. "They finally had to put her away. But I'd know those eyes anywhere. You've got 'em!"

Chapter 4

Although shaken by Aunt Prissy's remark, when Holly saw the dining room, she determined to enjoy her dinner. After all, this might be the only formal meal of her lifetime at Lyon House.

The room's oak-paneled walls were lined with family portraits, each individually lighted. Ornate silver candelabra cast a soft glow on the polished table, which was set with white mats, gold-rimmed plates, blue crystal glasses, and a bewildering array of Victorian silverware. Saito stood at a sideboard deftly opening two kinds of wine.

Carlotta directed Craig to the head of the table and settled herself at the foot. Holly sat at Craig's left, with Mimi next to her; Gay on Craig's right, then Tyler, and finally Aunt Prissy.

"Feels strange to be sitting at Dad's place," Craig remarked.

Aunt Prissy smacked her lips over the chilled lobster bisque. "After your mother died, *I* used to sit where Carlotta is now."

"Let's drink a toast," Craig lifted his wine glass. "Here's to an intriguing summer as a reunited family." He glanced intimately at Holly, his angular features romantically softened by the candlelight.

"Now to Archibald," said Aunt Prissy, raising her glass alone.

"Does anyone know," Mimi said, "if we actually have to spend every night all summer under this roof?"

"The only excuse for non-residency shall be hospitalization," Tyler quoted from the will.

As his sister's face fell, Carlotta asked quickly, "Where were you planning to go, dear?"

Mimi shrugged, "To visit friends in New York."

"She's a junior at Sarah Lawrence," Tyler explained to Gay.

These Lyon cousins were obviously no dummies, Holly

20

thought. Mimi was young to be a college junior, and Tyler was at the University of Virginia.

After the soup, Saito served individual steaks surrounded by plump mushroom caps.

"Yummy. Filet mignon," Aunt Prissy exclaimed.

"Lyon House has always served gourmet food," Tyler told Gay. "Order what you like for breakfast."

"Eggs benedict, smoked salmon, glazed doughnuts, and a cup of hot chocolate," said Gay promptly, smacking her hands on her knees, and obviously enjoying her role as an elegant guest.

"Canadian bacon for me," said Craig. "Dad always kept plenty in the freezer."

"Things have changed, I'm afraid," Carlotta told him, as Su Chen served puffed potato balls, spinach soufflé, and Belgian carrots. "The freezer's empty."

"Call Meade's Market tomorrow morning," Craig said.

"I already did," Carlotta said. "Archibald's charge account is closed."

Craig spooned butter sauce over his carrots. "Well, reopen it. We've used Meade's ever since I was a kid."

Carlotta shook her head. "Dodd closed the account. Orders from your father. Meade refused to open a new one. And, would you believe that the entire Lyon House pantry is empty? There aren't even any cans of food!"

"The Last Supper," Mimi murmured.

Craig glanced first at Saito, who was calmly pouring red wine for everyone; then he stared down the long table at his sister-in-law. "How the hell are we supposed to eat?"

Carlotta shrugged. "I don't know."

"Aren't there any supermarkets around here?" Holly asked, baffled when the whole family gaped at her.

"Supermarkets want cold, hard cash," Mimi said bluntly.

"Doesn't anybody have any *money?*" Gay gasped.

A hush fell over the dining table, broken finally by Craig. "Let's put our cards on the table. I'm nearly flat. I wrote Dad from Spain to send next year's allowance early, but he never got around to answering."

"I bank in London," said Carlotta, "and my account over there is a bit low."

"I'm down to eight dollars and fifty-seven cents," Mimi announced.

Tyler glanced uncomfortably at Gay. "Should we discuss this in front of a guest?"

"Please do," Gay said. "I'm fascinated."

"Just don't tell Caddy," he muttered, his face red.

"It's reality, *dear*," Mimi told her brother sarcastically. "None of us can survive if we don't eat. Knowing you, I'm sure you're broke. How's your bread box, Holly? Loaded?"

Holly shook her head. "I have to earn money this summer for school."

Mimi snorted. "Well, folks, we'll *all* have to earn our way on this trip."

"You mean *work?*" Tyler sounded horrified.

"That's how most people earn," Mimi said drily. "Or hadn't you heard?"

"But how will we get jobs?" Tyler asked. "Grandfather's dead."

His sister snickered. "That's the whole point."

"I mean," said Tyler, "we can't get him to fix us up with his friends."

"How about the Help Wanted ads in your local paper?" Gay asked.

"They only list menial jobs like mowing lawns and delivering groceries," Tyler said.

"The pay's pretty good for jobs like those up home," said Holly.

Tyler dabbed at his mouth with his meticulously ironed napkin. "I'm a Lyon. What would people say?"

"Knock it off," Mimi snapped. "That image bit went out twenty years ago. Mess up your elegant threads for a change."

"Just because you've turned into a phony liberal doesn't mean *I* have to!" Tyler retorted, his blue eyes blazing.

"Children!" Carlotta cried. "Quarreling won't solve our dilemma!"

"We need cash," Craig announced. "Not only for food, but also to run this place. Electricity, water, telephone—"

"Servants," said Aunt Prissy.

"Grandfather left wages for Saito and Su Chen," Tyler reminded her.

"When my brother Edward died five years ago," said Craig slowly, "he didn't exactly leave you a poor woman, Carlotta."

"Nor a rich one," she said quickly. "My income barely covers our living expenses. Archibald always paid for tuitions and vacations. He hadn't sent our summer check this year, which is why I'm low now. But what about you, Craig? Didn't your father give you an ample allowance?"

Craig looked uncomfortable. "I traveled a lot last year. The Greek Islands, Spain. I've never had any need to save."

"Then we'll start being practical," Carlotta said. "How do you suppose one job-hunts around here?"

"Did Dad still own the *Laurel Cove Gazette*?" Craig asked.

Aunt Prissy nodded. "I have a subscription."

"Good. I'll sign on tomorrow for the summer."

"What's the *Gazette*?" Gay asked him.

"A weekly newspaper. My grandfather founded it. Dad hung on to it mainly for a hobby."

"Are you a reporter?" Holly asked.

Craig nodded. "Strictly free lance. I was on the Harvard *Crimson*. Worked at the *Gazette* a couple of summers during college, and do an occasional article for them if I'm here. I contribute to English-language papers abroad." He grinned. "Normally I'm a roving reporter, but now it looks as if I'll have to be a full-time one—for the summer, anyway."

"I write," Holly surprised herself by saying.

"Do you?" Craig regarded her with interest.

"I did several articles for the school newspaper last semester," she said.

"They were super!" Gay said. "Her journalism professor gave her an 'A' for a series she did on hospitals."

"Journalism runs in the family," Aunt Prissy remarked. "Your mother was a reporter, Holly."

"Really?" Holly was startled. Grandpa Blake had never mentioned this. In fact, he'd barely glanced at Holly's articles, growling that her grades were down, and she'd "better study instead of wastin' time" or she'd lose her teacher-trainee scholarship.

23

"I remember the summer Julia worked on the *Gazette*," Aunt Prissy continued. "She was your age, Holly. Had a lively mind and liked tracking down an exciting story. But she couldn't handle . . ." The old lady's voice trailed off and she forked up several Belgian carrots.

"Couldn't handle what?" Tyler asked.

"Certain things." His great-aunt pointed her fork at a formal portrait of a lady with an upswept hairdo. "Just like my aunt over there. *Your* great-grandmother." She saluted Holly with the fork before turning back to her meal.

"Holly seems pretty capable to me," Craig told her. "Would you like a cub reporting job at the paper, Holly?"

His lopsided grin appeared. Holly's heart beat faster, and not just because of the job. She was drawn to him, but wondered how much of that feeling was real and how much was due to the cocktails, the wine, and the elegant, candlelit atmosphere.

"You'd be a *fool* to pass that up!" said Gay enthusiastically. "You really liked that journalism course, and now you know where your writing talent comes from—the Lyons."

"But I'm also a Blake, remember?" Holly argued weakly. "So, teaching school is also my heritage."

Gay made a face. "You know, you've been more and more turned off this year by the idea of teaching."

Holly nodded. Her friend was right. Here was a perfect chance to try a new career. She turned to Craig. "Could I earn enough by the end of the summer to cover a partial tuition payment?"

Craig frowned. "Cub reporting is a low-paying apprenticeship."

"And you'll have to chip in for living expenses," Tyler said.

Gay leaned forward. "Holly's a crack secretary," she told Craig. "Good secretaries are hard to find."

Craig beamed at her. "That's the ticket! You could work as a secretary and train as a cub, Holly, and we'd be at the *Gazette* together. Sound like fun?"

Holly felt herself nod assent.

"So you'll stay for the summer?" Carlotta asked.

"Please do." Craig's brown eyes were fixed on Holly—those eyes so like her mother's.

"Two contestants thus in allegiance," Tyler said. "Very

clever ploy, Craig. Can't I persuade you to work with me, Holly?"

"Doing what?" Holly asked, and Mimi hooted with laughter.

Tyler's face turned red. "What job do you think *you'll* find, sister dear?"

Mimi gazed evenly at him. "I'll manage." She spoke in such a calm voice that Holly was surprised to notice her cousin's fists—clenched so tightly in her lap the knuckles were white.

"There are all kinds of household details to consider," said Carlotta briskly. "Heavy cleaning, laundry, the grounds. . . ."

Craig burst out laughing. "Don't be ridiculous, Carlotta! Those things cost *money*!" He drained his wine glass and signaled to Saito for a refill. "My father must have been out of his mind!"

"Your father was quite rational, let me assure you, Craig." Aunt Prissy's hoarse voice shook with emotion.

"Was he?" Craig's voice had a bitter edge. "His will sounds to me like some kind of crazy kindergarten joke."

"Do we all agree that Grandfather was whacked out two summers ago?" Tyler asked eagerly.

Craig nodded, but Holly thought of Archibald's letter, which hardly seemed irrational to her.

Tyler leaned forward, his blue eyes gleaming oddly in the candlelight. "We *all* know Grandfather behaved insanely at times. If we could prove he was mentally incompetent, we could break that will wide open. What do you say, Mother? After all, you're not even included."

Aunt Prissy slammed her wine glass down so hard the stem snapped off. "Tyler Lyon, you're a naughty, naughty boy!" she shouted. "My brother Archibald was no more insane than I am!" She waved the broken glass at him, ignoring the crimson stain spreading across her white table mat.

Saito quickly removed the old lady's mat and glass, while Su Chen cleared away the plates. Although their faces were composed, Holly wondered if the pair had understood any of the conversation. And, if so, were they shocked? Had Archibald Lyon been a difficult boss?

"It's expensive to contest a will, Tyler," said Carlotta. "We can't afford it."

25

"The money's there. We just can't get our hands on it," Tyler fumed.

After dinner, Gay and Tyler went out. Mimi went up to her room. The others gathered in the library, but the unaccustomed number of drinks had made Holly sleepy, so she decided to go to bed.

Craig followed her into the hall. "Are you staying for the summer?" he asked, taking her hand.

Holly felt a wave of desire for him. "I think so," she whispered, then ran upstairs.

On the vanity in her room, she found an old dresser set that had not been there before dinner. The initials 'J.L.' were carved on the ivory backs.

Julia Lyon!

It must have belonged to her mother. Was this also, she wondered with rising excitement, her mother's room? She hugged the brush to her cheek, trying to picture her mother right here, getting ready for bed.

But was her mother's hair long or short? Dark or blonde? It was no use. Holly couldn't remember.

She laid down the brush and noticed a bud vase containing a single yellow rose. This, too, had not been here before dinner. Tied around the flower was a typed letter, dated January 8, fourteen years ago. Exactly one month before Holly's parents died.

> Julia's recent paranoid delusions prove that she is incapable of coping with reality.
> Her latest traffic violation and her reaction to it are further proof of her instability.
> I strongly recommend sending her to a good hospital like Thompson.

The signature was torn off, but the writer had added a P.S. in ink:

> Caution Julia that this is a hereditary disease, should she ever be well enough to have another child.

The color drained from Holly's face. Who left this letter with the perfect yellow rose? The same person who hid behind the yellow rosebush and hurled that boulder at her? She sank into the rocking chair, as the pink and white walls of the room seemed to close in on her. The plaintive call of a seagull intensified her fear. How could she bear three months in this house with an unknown enemy?

She leaped to her feet. Nobody was forcing her to stay! She'd leave Lyon House at once! Phone for a taxi, take a train to New York, and then a bus home to Vermont.

And let her foe get rid of her this easily? The very first day of the three-month period?

Still high from all the drinks, she tried to think rationally. Someone wanted to scare her away. Did the enemy plan to frighten off each contestant in turn?

She began to get angry, thinking of reasons to stay at Lyon House: She had been offered a great-sounding job. By an extremely attractive—if enigmatic—man. She could find out how her parents died and what had been wrong with her mother. She could look for what Cousin Archibald said was "rightfully hers." And, last but not least, she could compete for the estate, which might open doors to a new life she had never before dared even dream about!

She would be a fool to *leave!*

For all his faults, Grandpa Blake was a fighter. Holly was, too, and the drinks seemed to give her extra courage. She'd call home and break the news tonight, before she lost her nerve.

She remembered seeing a telephone alcove downstairs, off the entrance hall. Enclosed by a velvet drapery, Holly snapped on a wall sconce, dialed, and moments later, Grandpa Blake's rage crackled three hundred and fifty miles over the wires from northern Vermont.

"I refused to tell that shyster lawyer where you were. How'd he find you?"

"At college." Holly spoke carefully, hoping her teetotaling grandfather wouldn't realize that she'd been drinking.

"How 'bout the drugstore?" Grandpa demanded. "Not easy to get a girl to work the counter who knows books, too. Summer folks've arrived. We're mighty busy."

"I've been offered a job on the family newspaper," Holly told him. When he snorted, she added, "Grandpa, I'm as much a Lyon as a Blake, you know."

The instant the words were out, she realized what a terrible mistake they were.

"The Lyons are crazy, Holly!" he shouted. "They'll corrupt you! Look what happened to your Pa!"

"Grandpa," she said quietly, "it's not my fault Pa died here. But just because he did, it's not fair of you to keep me away from Lyon House. Archibald Lyon left me a letter." She gripped the envelope for moral support. "A beautiful letter."

"Talk's cheap," he muttered. "What'd the old tyrant say?"

"He wanted me to spend the summer here."

"That's what Jack told me twenty-one years ago," he said. "Grandma and I only want to save you from what happened to our boy Jack."

She closed her eyes as she thought of her grandmother's face, rough and worn as the rugged country she'd lived in all her life. Holly hated to hurt these old people who had done so much for her, but the pull of her Lyon heritage was too powerful to resist. "I'm twenty now, and I have to start finding things out for myself. I'm sorry, Grandpa."

"You'll be *dang* sorry!" he shouted. "I'll bet you're just a pawn. But, if you're bent on bein' stubborn, I'll send your clothes down. You better stand by your decision!" Without saying goodbye, he crashed down his receiver.

Holly slumped in the alcove, blinking back tears. Where would she go if life became unbearable for her here?

Suddenly she heard footsteps. "Does somebody want to use the phone?" she called, parting the curtains.

No one answered. The vast hall was pitch black, except for the spotlit statue of the praying hands.

Stealthy footsteps moved along a wall. Holly tensed. "Who's there?" she called, louder this time.

Still no response. Was that soft breathing behind a Japanese screen? Fear prickled along her spine. She snapped off the wall sconce and closed the curtains, listening intently.

The old house was absolutely silent, as if waiting with Holly . . . for what?

Then it started.

A slow, soft whistling . . . expertly warbled . . . the long notes echoing faintly in the huge hall. Holly recognized the familiar Christmas carol at once:

The Holly and the Ivy . . .
When they are both full-grown . . .
Of all the trees that are in the wood,
The Holly stands alone!

She huddled behind the soft velvet, fingers cold with terror, breathing shallow. Although the phone was at her elbow, whom could she call for help? If the police came to this grand estate, wouldn't the family tell them that Holly's mind was unbalanced like her mother's? That this very afternoon she'd "imagined" a boulder aimed at her?

The whistling started again, softer and slower this time:

Of all the trees that are in the wood,
The Holly stands alone!

As the final note died poignantly in the still night air, something thumped nearby.

With a yelp of alarm, Holly dashed up the staircase and down the long corridor to her room. Only when she was in her nightgown did she notice that, although the yellow rose was still on her vanity table, the letter about her mother that had been tucked around the vase was gone.

In addition, her room had been searched.

Chapter 5

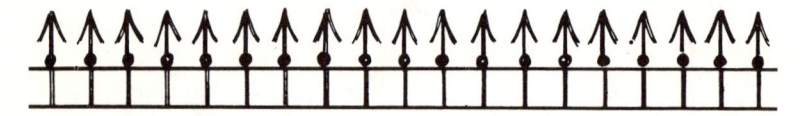

The next morning, awakened by a quartet of robins, Holly breathed the salty air, saw Laurel Harbor sparkling in the June sunshine, and decided that last night seemed like a bad dream. Almost.

She found Gay alone in the dining room. The only food in sight was a silver yachting trophy filled with brown speckled eggs.

"Read this." Gay chuckled as she handed Holly a note propped against the bowl.

> Dear Family:
> Breakfast is on me this morning.
> Am out job hunting. See you tonight.
>   Mimi

"Saito will fix your eggs, but there's nothing to go with them," Gay said.

"Have a good time last night?" Holly asked.

Gay made a face. "When Tyler found out that Pop's a construction worker and Mom's a telephone operator, it was all over for us."

"Was he with you all evening?" Holly asked.

Gay nodded. "Except to phone some friend in Virginia. Hey—you asked me that same question yesterday. What's up?"

Holly lowered her voice. "Somebody's trying to scare me away from here."

"Not Tyler. He's basically too insecure. But he mentioned that you think someone tossed a rock at you. I told him you have a very frisky imagination."

"It happened!" Holly protested. "And last night, while I phoned Grandpa, someone was there listening. And whoever it was kept on whistling 'The Holly and the Ivy.'"

Gay laughed. "This house looks made for ghosts. I'll bet if you whistle in one room, the sound echoes in another."

"Then how would you explain the 'gift' of a yellow rose, when that rock was thrown from behind the only yellow rose bush? Or a letter which someone removed while I was downstairs talking to—"

"Calm down, Holly," said Gay. "In big fancy houses like this, servants go into people's bedrooms all the time. Wasn't your bed turned down last night?"

Holly nodded.

"Su Chen probably did her number while you were downstairs. I found roses in my room, too."

"Red or yellow?"

"Red, but so what? It's just coincidence you got yellow."

"Morning, girls." Craig stood in the door, holding the Siamese cat. "I found Gning playing with a dead mouse. Near the phone alcove," he added, glancing at Holly.

While Gay greeted Craig, Holly stared uneasily at him. He would know about last night's thump if he was the whistler.

"Didn't mean to scare you, Holly." Dropping the animal with a final pat, Craig strode to the table as Saito appeared in the swinging door to the kitchen. "Good morning, Saito. Great—fresh eggs. Scramble me three, please? A large tomato juice, rye toast, lightly buttered, and coffee with heavy cream."

Gay hid a smile as the houseman said, "No toast, sir. No butter. No tomato juice. No coffee."

Craig's jaw dropped. "I forgot. Can you scramble eggs without butter?"

31

Saito shook his head. Holly suggested, "How about boiled?"

Craig wrinkled his nose. "At least we have water. And maybe I can rustle up some juice from the bar."

When the girls were alone again, Gay said, "Holly, you'll never make it here if you're suspicious all the time. These people may seem bent out of shape sometimes, but I think they're basically okay. You should stick around. Learn newspaper work, and have your shot at the estate."

"I told Grandpa last night I'd stay," Holly said ruefully. "So I guess the die is cast."

Craig was back, holding aloft a bottle of Bloody Mary mix. "Look what I found! And Bremen wafers to go with our boiled eggs."

When Gay left after breakfast, Craig suggested they go to the newspaper office. Holly's eyes widened at the four automobiles in the garage. "Did your father own all these?"

He opened the door of a metallic blue Porsche with beige leather seats. "Just the Mercedes. This one's mine, the Toyota's Saito's, and Tyler owns the E-type Jaguar."

As the low-slung sports car purred down the wooded driveway, Holly asked, "Do you know which room my mother used?"

"Yours," said Craig. "She called it the Rosebud Room, because of the rug. Did you know that your mother adored roses?"

"I'd forgotten." A faint memory stirred. "After she died, Grandpa uprooted all her bushes and threw them in the town dump. Were you here the night my parents died?"

Craig shook his head. "I was at boarding school."

Thinking of last night's letter, Holly watched his face intently. "Have you ever heard of Thompson Hospital?"

He shook his head again, but his eyes were inscrutable behind dark glasses. "Where is it?"

"Somewhere on Long Island," she said vaguely.

Craig parked behind a small, grey-shingled house at one end of Laurel Cove's quaint Main Street. Telling Holly that the *Gazette* owned the building, he seemed surprised that the first two floors were occupied by a real estate firm and a yacht brokerage. He led the way up two steep flights of stairs to the attic, which was divided into several offices.

"Is Mr. Russell here?" Craig asked a grey-haired man behind a cluttered desk.

"He's not with the *Gazette* any more," the man said. "Left two years ago. I'm Murray West, managing editor. Can I help you?"

"Yes. I'm Craig Lyon, Archibald's son."

Murray held out his hand. "My condolences about your father. Extraordinary man. What can I do for you?" He lit a cigarette.

"I'd like a reporting job," said Craig.

Murray exhaled a thin stream of smoke. "My reporters work a five-day week, from nine to five, plus any night assignments I want covered."

Craig laughed. "I'm hardly a cub. I've written on and off for the *Gazette* since Harvard days."

"I know. But I'd expect the same hours from you as from everyone else."

"Dad always paid me by the article," said Craig. "Top rates. Why don't we use the same deal?"

"This paper is twice the size it used to be because I run a tight ship," Murray told him. "Village weeklies can't make money giving free-lancers top rates. I pay twenty bucks an article."

"That's peanuts!"

"On the other hand, if you work full time, I'll pay you a hundred and fifty bucks a week. For that, I'll expect the hours I mentioned, and at least five articles each week."

"Dad always gave me any time off I wanted," Craig protested.

"Your father is no longer alive," Murray said.

"But I'm his *son*!" Craig exploded. "You can't treat me like some flunky who comes in off the street!"

"As managing editor, I can treat you any way I like," said Murray evenly.

Craig glared at him. "Do you own the *Gazette*?" When Murray shook his head, Craig snapped, "I'm going to call my lawyer." He strode into another office and slammed the door.

"You must be Holly. What can I do for you?" Murray asked.

"I'd like to apply for a job, too," she said uneasily. "But as a secretary. I type eighty words a minute, my shorthand's a hundred and twenty. I worked part-time last year for a professor at Vermont Teacher's College."

"It so happens we need a secretary," he said. "Any newspaper experience?"

"Two journalism courses, and I wrote a few articles for the school paper. I was hoping," she hesitated, "though it's not necessary, that I could train as a cub reporter. On my own time."

"Sure. We're small enough so everyone doubles up. I'll pay you a hundred bucks a week. You can start right now."

Holly barely reached her desk in the reception room before the phones began to ring. The first caller wanted to announce a garage sale for the benefit of the village Boy Scouts. Murray explained the newspaper's style and showed her a row of wooden boxes for the typesetter. As she filed her short article under Club News, she heard Craig's voice raised in anger.

"Okay. You have full control of the *Gazette* for three months. But I'm warning you, Murray, after the paper reverts back to my family. . . ."

Holly missed the rest because her phone rang. When she finished the call, Craig was standing at her desk. "Don't take this job if you don't want it," he said in a low voice. "Murray's running the paper like boot camp. Hardly the 'fun' I mentioned last night."

"Are you staying?" Holly asked.

He nodded. "To find out what's going on. Why, for example, did Dad hire that Captain Queeg type? He just claimed that Dad worked here full time. What a liar!"

"Could it be true?" Holly asked.

Craig gestured impatiently. "Dad never worked full time at *anything*. The *Gazette* was one of his hobbies—he never gave a damn whether or not the paper made money. I think Murray's pulling a fast one—playing tough to keep me out. But it won't work."

As Murray came in with bills for Holly to type and articles for Craig to edit, Craig murmured quickly, "I'll take you to lunch at the Yacht Club. Cheer us both up."

The invitation was unexpected, coming after his angry outburst. Holly wished she could run home and change into something more dressy. Could his appeals to her to remain at Lyon House be based on a romantic interest?

At noon, someone asked loudly, "Is Craig Lyon here?"

Holly glanced up from her typewriter at a tall woman in her middle twenties. Her immaculate white tennis outfit accentuated her deep tan and tawny-streaked hair. "He's on the phone," Holly said. "If you'd like to wait out here, I'll—"

But the beautiful stranger strode past her and opened the door to the middle office. "Craig, darling!" she cried.

"Hello, Audrey!"

Holly watched with dismay as the woman bent down and kissed Craig lingeringly on the lips.

Chapter 6

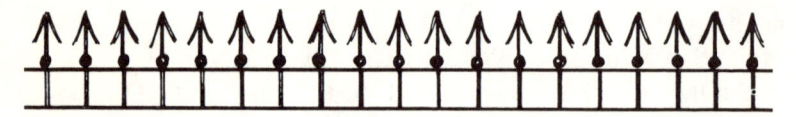

Audrey Woodward, society reporter for the *Gazette*, acknowledged her introduction to Holly with a cool, bored nod. But when Craig added, "Holly's my cousin," her hazel eyes flicked over every detail of Holly's wrap skirt, T-shirt, and inexpensive clogs.

"Nice meeting you, Polly. Craig, sweetie. . . ." She caught his hand. "Let's run over to the Club for a drink and a bite of lunch. I'm absolutely wilting from this heat."

Holly held her breath as Craig wiped his perspiring face. Would he remember *their* date? "I sure could use a drink," he said. "But I already asked—"

"I'm doing a story on the racing season," Audrey cut in quickly. "I need your help with those beastly technical details." Holly winced as Audrey swung Craig's hand teasingly back and forth.

"Do you mind, Holly?" Craig asked. "Since it's business."

Holly tried to look noncommittal. "Not a bit," she lied.

Heading downstairs, Craig told Audrey, "I can't wait to see what shape *Lady Lyon's* in. Tyler and I want to sail her."

"Didn't you know your father sold the boat?" Audrey asked. "But, honey, anytime you want to sail on *Aristocrat*, just give me a call. . . ."

Murray went to lunch, leaving Holly alone at the *Gazette*.

About a half hour later, a sandy-haired boy in jeans loped up the steps.

"Are you waiting for somebody?" he asked, carefully laying an expensive camera on her desk.

Holly shook her head. "I just started working here. I'm Holly Blake."

"Peter Meade, staff photographer and sometime reporter." He was about her age, and although not as handsome as the Lyon men, he had friendly grey eyes behind tortoise-shell rimmed glasses. "Did Mr. Lyon hire you before he died?"

Holly shook her head again. "He was a distant cousin, but Murray gave me the job."

Peter looked puzzled. "Mr. Lyon never mentioned you."

"My mother was his ward—Julia Lyon Blake."

"Never heard of her either. Say—take a look at this." He opened a manila envelope and drew out an eight-by-ten glossy photograph of an old man with white hair, a moustache, and a gentle smile.

"He looks nice," said Holly. "Who is he?"

Peter's eyes widened. "Who *is* he? What's with *you*, Holly? That's Archibald Lyon! Posed for me last month."

Now Holly could see the surface resemblance to the portrait at Lyon House. But here he had kind eyes with a twinkle in them. "You made him look like a wonderful old man," she said softly.

"He was." Peter's voice was husky. "We were real buddies. Didn't you think he was super?"

"I never met him."

"World's greatest boss. Nobody had to do one caper that he wouldn't do himself. Worked a ten-hour day—at age seventy-five! I never dreamed his health was a bummer."

Holly was perplexed. Mr. Dodd, Murray, and now Peter, had all admired Archibald Lyon.

Could they, as Craig suggested, have an ulterior motive regarding the *Gazette*?

Peter invited Holly to join him for lunch. "There's a burger place down the block. My dad owns it. All the locals chow there, so it's great for catching village news."

At the crowded Hamburg Nook, Peter introduced Holly to his father, Royal Meade.

"Welcome to Laurel Cove." Stout and balding, Mr. Meade wiped his huge hand on a towel and enveloped her small hand in his. "Call me Royal. Your Cousin Arch was a real good friend of mine. We used to fish together for hours off his beach. Goin' to miss him somethin' terrible."

Evidently Archibald Lyon hadn't followed the family standards for snobbery. "What was his favorite lunch?" Holly asked Royal.

"Rare hamburger with melted cheddar, bacon, sweet pickles, and pimiento, and a thick mocha shake." He grinned, revealing several gold teeth. "Ordered it just two weeks ago. Ate the whole thing, too."

"I'll try it," she told him.

Peter circulated through the crowded restaurant, stopping at almost every booth to pick up local news, or to introduce Holly to people. After the put-down from Audrey Woodward and the broken lunch date, Holly was glad to be in this noisy, friendly atmosphere.

They found two stools at the counter. Despite his bulk, Royal took orders and tended the sizzling grill swiftly, but serenely. Several times, Holly saw him point in her direction and say, "That's Mr. Lyon's young cousin," or "That's Archie's kin," then make introductions. When Holly and Peter prepared to leave, he added, "Any time you got a problem, come see me."

"Thanks," Holly said, "Your food's delicious."

He winked. "Not as fancy as Lyon House, but Arch sure liked it. Ate here nearly every day."

Peter went off to Town Hall on a story. At three-thirty, Murray was dictating a letter to Holly when Craig returned with Audrey. Both were in obvious high spirits.

"Around here lunch hour is just that—one hour," Murray said.

"Oh, Murray, do you have to be picayune on such a heavenly June day?" Audrey asked.

"You free lance," said Murray. "Craig's on staff. Out for three and a half hours. I had to send our photographer on a Town Hall story."

"Why didn't you tell me before I left?" Craig sounded annoyed.

"The call came in at one-fifteen. I didn't know how to reach you," Murray said.

Afraid that Craig might lose his temper again and quit, Holly said quickly, "I knew where they were, Murray. I should have told you."

"It's Craig's responsibility to call in," said Murray coldly.

"I hadn't been at the Yacht Club in two years," Craig explained. "It was like old home week."

I'll bet, Holly thought, as Audrey smiled radiantly.

"However," Craig continued, "I heard some hot news. The mayor of Laurel Cove has decided not to run for re-election."

"Really?" Murray grabbed pencil and paper off Holly's desk. "Why not?"

"He's going for state senate instead. I heard his brother talking about it."

As he headed for a phone, Murray said, "Just what we need for this week's front page lead."

At five o'clock, Craig seemed gloomy as he and Holly left the office together. "There's so much variety at the *Gazette* I could never be bored," she said, trying to make conversation.

"It was a gas to work there when Dad was around," he said. "But the Lyons will get the paper back in three months, unless we're sabotaged in the meantime." He glanced at his watch. "Say—it's early. Shall we have a drink to celebrate our first day at work? Carlotta phoned. She bought food for dinner." He turned the Porsche into the parking lot of the Harbor Inn, a white Colonial building with green shutters.

From a dining terrace, Holly could see dozens of boats in Laurel Harbor: languid white sails interspersed with speed boats towing waterskiers. A perfect picture postcard of Long Island's North Shore at play, she thought, acutely aware of the handsome man across the table from her. How could she snap him out of his depression?

"I met some of your father's friends today at the Hamburg Nook," she said.

"Probably just acquaintances," said Craig. "Dad always ate lunch at the Club, or at home."

Holly shook her head. "Not recently. These guys knew him pretty well."

"They were putting you on. You'll have to learn not to be naive, Holly. Dad had a lot of money, you know. Certain types will try any gambit to get to know you."

"Maybe he changed," she suggested, thinking of Peter's complimentary remarks.

Craig shook his head. "Dad was too arrogant and too old. However. . . ." He lowered his voice. "If you show me his letter, I can figure out why he set up such a weird will. I knew him better than anyone else."

Holly wondered uneasily if his interest in her was based on seeing that letter. It was zipped in the safety compartment of her bag, which she'd kept by her side all day. "I can't show it to anyone until the end of the summer."

"What makes you so bloody *furtive* about it?" Craig demanded.

Holly stared at him in consternation.

"The competition for Dad's estate is supposed to be fair!" he continued angrily. "But you, a total stranger, were given special treatment. Why, Holly? *Why?*" He leaned across the table, his brown eyes probing hers.

"I don't know!" she cried.

"Then tell me what secret Dad told you! I'll bet he told you something to help you win, didn't he?"

Holly jumped to her feet. "Please take me home."

He rose at once. "Sorry . . . My nerves are shot." He shook his head as if to clear it. "Forgive me?" Now his eyes were pleading, and as a waitress approached with their drinks, he added, "Please stay? I promise to be nice."

Holly wavered, still drawn to him.

"You must be curious about your mother's side of the family," he said. "Ask me anything you want."

Holly sat down again. She had spotted Lyon House a few minutes before, proudly isolated on its high cliff across the harbor. "How long has your family owned Lyon House?"

"It's been in the family over seventy years, first as a summer place," he said. "Long Island was still real country then."

Although Laurel Cove was a rapidly growing suburban community over forty miles from New York City, Holly knew that the estate included hundreds of acres.

"When Dad retired from Wall Street fifteen years ago," Craig continued, "we started living here year round."

"Were you lonely?"

He nodded. "No friends within easy walking distance. I went to boarding school at eleven. My brother Edward—Carlotta's late husband—was fifteen years older, so I was like an only child."

"I know how lonely that can be," Holly said softly. "I hear your father enjoyed fishing. Do you?"

Craig looked startled. "Dad never fished. He always said sitting that still in a boat made him nervous."

Although Royal had mentioned fishing with Archibald off the Lyon beach, Holly didn't want to annoy Craig again, just when she was beginning to feel comfortable with him. "Has Aunt Prissy always lived at Lyon House?" she asked.

"No," said Craig. "She has an apartment in New York, near the girls' school where she taught sports, but she's usually here Christmases and summers. She was the only Lyon to see Dad during the last two years."

Holly spotted a station wagon turning into the parking lot. Mimi emerged with a bearded redhead who wore oddly greenish cowboy boots with high heels. Both were laughing as he hoisted a crate from the car.

"Look at Mimi," Holly said. "She's actually laughing!"

"Moody kid," Craig said. "Gives Carlotta a tough time."

"Why doesn't she go along with society life, like Tyler?" Holly asked, as the boy headed for the kitchen area with the crate.

Craig laughed. "God knows. I'll never forget the summer Mimi was twelve. Carlotta had signed up both kids for the Country Club dancing classes. Tyler shot into his party clothes like a greased streak, but Mimi refused to go. She got so whipped up that she tried to push her mother down the stairs. Damn near succeeded, too—crazy kid!"

He chuckled, but Holly did not. His light use of the word "crazy" reminded her of Grandpa Blake's claim that all the Lyons were crazy. As Craig ordered another round of drinks, she asked, "What happened to your brother?"

"Edward died five years ago. Pneumonia. They were living in London. Heck of a nice guy, but Carlotta twisted him around her little finger. Edward loved Lyon House, but she always wanted to live abroad."

Now Holly wondered why Carlotta had tangled with Cousin Archibald two years ago. Why had she stopped bringing his only grandchildren here, especially since the old man had underwritten their school tuitions and summer vacations?

After the second drink, they drove home. Craig now seemed so relaxed, even attentive, that, despite Audrey Woodward, Holly again began to hope for a romance.

As she changed into a clean shirt, Holly hoped her grandparents had packed the few dressy clothes she owned. She arrived downstairs slightly early for dinner. The entrance hall was deserted. Thinking of Archibald's reference to a clue in the ninth step, she mounted back up nine steps, stooped, and examined the stair in the dim light of a wall sconce. It was covered with a thick, maroon-colored carpet, which was tucked firmly in place. She'd need a claw hammer to investigate further.

Next, she ran her fingers over the carved banister posts on that step. They seemed solid, with no cracks to indicate a hiding place. Bending to peer under the banister rail, she heard a noise above her head.

She dashed down and was examining the statue of the praying hands when a hoarse voice rasped, "Don't ever touch those hands!"

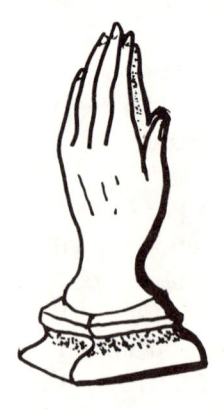

Holly whirled around. Aunt Prissy was descending the staircase. Had she seen Holly checking out the ninth step?

"Archibald treasured that statue," the old lady said solemnly. "It guards this house against evil." She pushed her lined face close to Holly's. "If anything ever happens to it, a Lyon will suffer! As your mother did with your father!" Her eyes glinted diabolically in the harsh glare of the spotlight.

"What do you mean?" Holly whispered.

"Death, my child. Death!"

Chapter 7

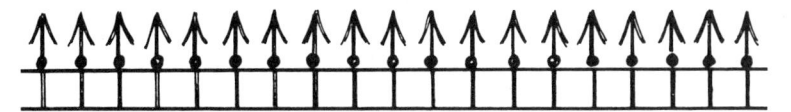

As Holly wondered uneasily if Aunt Prissy's mind was unbalanced, Saito announced dinner.

Plump shrimp nestled in silver bowls of cracked ice at each place.

"Quite an improvement over breakfast," Craig remarked. "Did Meade change his mind about letting us charge?"

Carlotta shook her head. "I gave the delivery boy a check. But let's discuss that later. Did anyone land a job?"

"Holly and me," Craig said. "We're both at the *Gazette*."

"How grand!" Aunt Prissy said warmly. "Archibald took a sudden interest in the paper recently. He'd be delighted that another young Lyon shows journalistic aptitude." She beamed at Holly, as if her warning in the hall had never taken place.

"The new managing editor is a real s.o.b.," said Craig. "Treats me like a factory worker. Practically makes me punch a time clock."

"What nerve!" said Carlotta. "Doesn't he know who you are?"

Craig nodded.

"Why don't you fire him?"

"I wish I could. But Dad gave him control of the paper for the summer."

"Another sign," said Tyler, "that Grandfather was off his rocker."

"Better keep an eye on the man," Carlotta told Craig, as Saito brought in an enormous roast beef. "Mimi, how did you spend your day, dear?"

"Working at a farm stand."

Carlotta looked startled, but Aunt Prissy said, "Nice, healthy job. Did you hunt for employment, too, Tyler?"

43

He shook his head. "Mother asked me to help her organize the household," he said self-importantly. "We asked Mr. Dodd to look up Grandfather's operating expenses. Then we drew up a budget for this summer. Shall I read it now?" he asked Carlotta.

"You might as well, dear."

Tyler consulted a sheet of paper. "These figures are by the month: Electricity four hundred dollars. Telephone seventy-five. Oil one-twenty-five. Water pump twenty-five. Gardening service four hundred. Food: we figured about fifteen hundred including liquor. Dry cleaning a hundred. Miscellaneous seventy-five. That comes to a total of two thousand four hundred dollars per month."

Someone whistled softly.

"I divided that by six," Tyler continued. "So each person contributes four hundred a month."

"Does it really cost that much to run Lyon House?" Holly asked in an awed voice.

Carlotta spooned hollandaise sauce over her fresh asparagus. "Lyon House isn't a cottage in the mountains, dear."

Holly did some rapid mental calculations. After taxes, her one-hundred-dollar-a-week salary wouldn't be enough. She gazed around the table in consternation. How would the others handle it? Would they draw on savings, or sell stocks? She had neither, and Murray didn't seem like the type to give her a big raise on her second day of work.

When nobody voiced any objection to the proposed budget, she finally said hesitantly, "I—I can't afford that much."

"Each family member will contribute a proportionate share to household expenses." Tyler quoted the will as if he were a judge handing down a sentence.

Holly began to grow angry at Cousin Archibald. Why hadn't he anticipated this? If he was so anxious for his grand-niece to spend the summer in this extravagant mansion, why didn't he leave her at least *some* money to tide her over?

Mimi laid down her fork and knife. "I can't hack it either," she announced. "I'm only making ninety a week after taxes."

"Is your job part time?" Carlotta asked.

Mimi shook her head.

"Then why are they paying you so little?"

"They're not. Lots of people live on that, Mummy, but they don't use ripoff markets like Meade's."

"Meade's wouldn't cheat us," said Craig. "We've used them ever since I was a kid."

"Exactly why they *would* rip you off. You wouldn't know the difference." Mimi turned to Holly as if for confirmation.

Holly nodded, surprised at this unexpected side of a Lyon cousin.

"And what makes you such a big expert, after one day at some crummy fruit stand?" Tyler asked.

Mimi glared at him. "Frank's is not a crummy fruit stand! We have customers from all over Nassau County. Mummy, what did you pay for this Bibb lettuce?"

"I've no idea."

"Since it's out of season, probably ninety-eight cents a head," said Mimi. "Iceberg lettuce is forty-nine cents at our place."

"Don't be so petty," Tyler snapped. "A few pennies more for a really decent salad won't make that much difference."

"Are you kidding?" Holly cried. "Multiplied by thirty-one dinners a month, it will."

Mimi winked at Holly. Her smile transformed her into a very pretty girl.

"Let's talk turkey," Aunt Prissy suggested briskly. "How much can each of us afford to contribute to the household?"

"I have to save over half my salary," said Mimi.

"Whatever for?" Carlotta asked. "You mustn't be stingy at a time like this, dear."

"I'm saving for a—a car." The pout was back on Mimi's face, and again Holly saw her clench her fists under the table until the knuckles turned white.

Tyler leaned forward. "Forget it. If you clear ninety dollars and save fifty, that leaves only forty dollars a week for Lyon House."

"I can't afford any more than that either," said Holly quickly.

"I suppose you want a car, too?" Tyler asked.

Holly shook her head. "I have to save for college."

"Forty a week sounds jake to me," said Aunt Prissy. "Retired private school gym teachers don't get much of a pension, you know."

Tyler scribbled some figures. "If the three of you pay forty dollars apiece, that's only a hundred and twenty a week. We need six hundred!"

Craig cleared his throat. "Murray's got me on coolie wages. If I pay more than forty to the house, I won't be able to eat lunch at the Yacht Club. Or take a girl any place but a second-run movie theatre."

"We're up to a hundred and sixty a week, folks," Tyler announced.

"Mummy, why don't you make up the difference," Mimi suggested. "You're not renting any fancy Mediterranean pad this summer."

"Good idea," said Tyler. "You can ante up four hundred and forty dollars a week, can't you, Mom?"

Carlotta hesitated. "I'm afraid not. My expenses were horrendous this spring, and I was counting on Archibald to see you and Mimi and me through the summer."

"How much can you afford?" Mimi asked.

"Actually, I can't contribute any money. But I'll be happy to run Lyon House for all of you."

Tyler stared at her, aghast. "Are you broke?"

Carlotta nodded.

Aunt Prissy thumped her fork on the table. "Are you *flat* broke, Carlotta?"

"Yes, Aunt Prissy. I'm literally down to pocket money."

"What do you mean by 'pocket money?'" the old lady demanded. "And don't pussyfoot with me, Carlotta Francis Lyon!"

A flush stained Carlotta's smooth cheeks. "My normal personal expenses. The hairdresser, exercise class, bridge stakes, tennis lessons. . . ."

Aunt Prissy snorted. "That sounds like at *least* forty dollars a week—of self-indulgence."

"They're normal expenses!" Carlotta protested. "Every woman I know has them."

"*I* don't," said Aunt Prissy.

"Only the *rich* would consider them normal," Mimi said sarcastically. "What about getting a job, Mummy?"

"Me? Doing what?"

46

Her daughter shrugged. "Same type of thing as the rest of us working stiffs."

"It's either a job, Carlotta, or shampoo your own hair and exercise alone, as I do," Aunt Prissy said severely. "You'll contribute forty a week, same as everyone else."

Carlotta's hands flew up to her face. "Stop picking on me, all of you!" she cried. "This is a bloody nightmare! We can't live like welfare cases here! What the devil got into Archibald Lyon, anyway?"

She broke into loud, racking sobs. Tyler jumped up to comfort her. The rest of the family waited in uneasy silence as Saito and Su Chen cleared away the plates and brought in meringues with fresh, imported raspberries and real whipped cream.

"Take it easy, Carlotta. We're not on welfare yet." Craig jotted some figures on a pocket memo pad. "If everybody contributes forty a week, that's two forty a week total, or one thousand and sixty dollars a month. Not bad. Now—how do we shave thirteen hundred and forty off that budget?"

"Can we cut the gardening service?" Holly suggested.

"Why not? Let the grounds go for the summer," Mimi agreed.

But Aunt Prissy exclaimed in dismay. "Oh, no! Lyon House roses win prizes every year in the North Shore Garden Club Flower Show! My brother adored those roses, and his will says we should keep up the estate," she added inaccurately.

"Could we do the job ourselves?" Holly asked.

Aunt Prissy nodded vigorously, but Tyler shook his head. "It would take all day just to mow that front lawn," he said. "How can we do that, and work, too?"

Holly thought of home, where she and her grandparents ran the drugstore and did all the chores, and it never occurred to anyone to complain.

"If you don't want to pull your weight, Tyler, you can leave Lyon House," Aunt Prissy barked.

Carlotta gasped. Tyler glared at his great-aunt. "And lose my chance to win? Not a chance, Aunt Prissy! And you can't force me out of here!"

"Don't get fresh with me," Aunt Prissy said, so vehemently that Holly shivered in the warm night air.

"How do you feel about the grounds?" Mimi asked Craig. "After all, this is your childhood home."

He shrugged. "The roses are pretty, but frankly I'd rather do other things than garden in my spare time."

"In my home town," said Holly, "people hold what they call 'pruning days.' Every two weeks the whole family pitches in. One person mows the lawn, another rakes behind him, someone weeds, another prunes, and so on. It's really not so bad."

"And it's for free," Mimi pointed out.

"I'll tend the roses between times," Aunt Prissy volunteered.

"Is everyone in favor of family gardening as Holly suggested?" Craig asked.

When the whole family nodded, Aunt Prissy announced, "We just earned four hundred dollars."

And Holly realized that she would have an excuse to examine the stone steps in the formal garden for Cousin Archibald's mysterious clue.

"Nine hundred forty to go," said Craig. "The other big item is food. How can we cut down on that fifteen hundred a month, Carlotta?"

"I've no idea." Carlotta looked perplexed.

"First we quit using Meade's," Mimi said. "Agreed, Holly?"

Holly nodded. "Do you all eat like this every night?"

"Doesn't everyone?" Tyler asked.

Holly stifled a smile. "At home we have roast beef once a week, if that. No expensive appetizers unless it's a special occasion."

"What do you eat?" Tyler asked curiously.

"Things like stew, spaghetti, meat loaf, macaroni and cheese."

"I'm no truck driver, and I'm damned if I'll eat like one," Tyler growled.

"Cool it," his sister snapped. "I can buy vegetables at a good discount. If Su Chen cooks them Chinese style, and adds some of her wild sauces, we'll still eat well."

"We should use a supermarket," Holly added.

"Can you feed six, plus the servants, on sixty a month?" Tyler asked the girls.

"Are you out of your mind?" Mimi asked. "There should be

five hundred and sixty available for food. And don't forget household supplies."

Tyler shook his head. "We figured on five hundred for booze."

Holly couldn't believe her ears. "Five hundred dollars a month just for *liquor*?"

"We have a couple of cocktails apiece every evening," he told her. "That's at least a bottle, without guests. And two bottles of wine with dinner. Decent wine's not cheap."

"What about Dad's wine cellar?" Craig asked.

"It's empty," said Carlotta.

Craig's eyes widened. "What? He had hundreds of bottles down there! What happened to them?"

"Exactly what I'm wondering," said Tyler. "They must have been worth a fortune. Do you think Saito stole them?"

At that moment, Saito slid through the swinging door with more whipped cream. Holly winced, wondering again how much English he understood.

"Why don't we each buy our own booze?" Mimi suggested. "Since I'm not drinking these days, I'm in no mood to stand rounds for the whole gang anyway."

"And we'll save five hundred just like that!" Aunt Prissy snapped her fingers happily.

"Oh, boy! Bring your own bottle, just like a college dorm." Craig snorted. "Gracious living—goodbye. And Dad, wherever you are, go ahead and laugh! You've played one hell of a colossal joke on your family!" He jerked back his heavy chair, his jaw set in a tense line. "If you'll excuse me, I'm going out."

Although Saito brought a complete coffee service into the library, only Holly and Tyler wanted any. Mimi went out in the Mercedes, and Carlotta and Aunt Prissy went directly upstairs to bed.

Tyler settled into the big brown leather chair by the fireplace. "Gay called this afternoon," he said. "She's leaving for California tomorrow morning with her parents."

Holly suddenly wished that Gay were here now. She needed to talk to someone she could trust.

"She doesn't think you should be so secretive about

Grandfather's letter," said Tyler. "She suggested you share it with me."

Holly stared at him, stifling angry retorts, then jumped to her feet. "Sorry, Tyler, I'm beat. I'd better turn in."

He rose and bowed mockingly. "If you're thinking of waiting up for Craig, I wouldn't bother. The Woodwards live on the opposite side of the harbor. Pleasant *dreams*, dear cuz."

Holly fumed all the way upstairs. She found an old novel in her bookcase, but was too restless to read. She decided to take a walk. Changing into jeans and sneakers, she remembered about her room being searched the night before and tucked her cousin's letter in her pocket.

Tyler was still in the library, his gleaming blond head bent over a book. Holly tiptoed through the entrance hall and slipped out the front door.

The night was blanketed with fog. After yesterday's incident, she resolved to avoid the beach.

The crushed-gravel driveway ran steeply downhill from the house. At the bottom of the lawn, it turned and followed the craggy cliffs above the cove, crowded on the other side by deep woods. Trees and bushes dripped from the heavy mist, and the smell of pine in the damp air reminded Holly of Vermont. Aside from the mournful croaking of a frog and the muffled clanging of bell buoys in the harbor, the night was gloriously silent.

Holly walked briskly, feeling the tension literally drain out of her system. Until she heard the crunch of footsteps on the gravel behind her.

She halted, leaped over to the grass, and listened. Who knew she'd come out here? Had Tyler heard the click of the front door closing?

Swirling mists partially veiled the rhododendrons by the house. Was someone lurking behind that phantasmal foliage?

Poised for flight, Holly strained to hear the footsteps again. Had she imagined them? Or was it a small wild animal?

Crunch! . . . Crunch! . . . Crunch!

This was no small animal. It wore shoes, and was slowly approaching Holly along the gravel drive.

Despite her thumping heart, she tried not to panic. Couldn't it be just another family member out for an innocent evening stroll?

Crunch! . . . Crunch! . . . Crunch!

The small hairs on the back of her neck rose as she heard eerie music: the strains of that same Christmas Carol someone whistled last night in the front hall.

Only tonight, the tune was played on a harmonica.

> *The Holly and the Ivy . . .*
> *When they are both full grown . . .*
> *Of all the trees that are in the wood,*
> *The Holly stands alone . . .*

Goose pimples prickled Holly's arms as the notes trembled and died in the vaporous air. She was indeed alone tonight—more so than last night, since she was outdoors. If she tried to run, she could be trapped in the unfamiliar woods.

Mouth dry and hands icy, Holly tried desperately to see through the thick fog. She wished she had some sort of weapon, even a stout stick, but the grounds were too carefully tended for even a large stone to be lying about.

The footsteps continued at a relentlessly slow, measured tread.

Crunch! . . . Crunch! . . . Crunch!

Now they were mere yards away.

Crunch! . . . Crunch! . . . Crunch!

And another bar of harmonica music:

> *Of all the trees that are in the wood,*
> *The Holly stands alone . . .*

Panicked, she dove for the laurel bushes. The snapping of twigs sounded like thunder to her horrified ears, as she wiggled frantically through the wet, spikey leaves. A strip of grass edged the cliff, but it was only about five feet wide, and she could hear waves lapping on the beach a good fifty feet below her. She was thankful now for the fog, which should help to conceal her.

The nerve-wracking crunchings ceased. Had her pursuer heard her crash into the bushes? Was he, or she, hidden now on the other side of this hedge? Fully aware that Holly was trapped by the cliffs?

Suddenly she heard the faint hum of an automobile. Craig must be coming home! Flooded with relief, she almost leaped out, but decided to wait until the Porsche was abreast of her. Silently, she tucked Archibald's letter into her brassiere.

The car approached so slowly that Holly's panic rose in waves. Meanwhile, she forced herself to plan. The moment Craig's headlights pierced the fog, she would plunge through the bushes. Her enemy would have to slink off, and Holly could tell Craig everything.

Plagued by whining mosquitoes, she huddled deeper under the dripping laurel blossoms and tried not to think of the cliffs behind her. Any moment now, Craig's headlights would become visible, and she could leap to safety.

But—suddenly—strong arms in rubber sleeves grasped her around the waist, yanked her clear of the bushes, and clapped a cold, gloved hand over her mouth.

Chapter 8

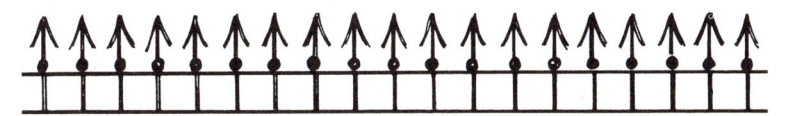

Holly was dragged behind the bushes, too near the cliff's edge to risk a struggle.

One hand still clamped on her mouth, the attacker whispered, "Where's the letter?" The hoarse whisper made it impossible to identify the voice.

If Holly refused, would she be shoved over the cliff? And then would a coroner's report state that she'd "stumbled in the foggy night and fallen to an accidental death"? Her offer to cooperate, however, was smothered by the rubber glove.

"Give it to me!" A hand clawed at Holly's pockets.

She squirmed, trying to free her mouth, yet terrified by the proximity of the precipice. Would Craig spot this silent battle behind the laurel bushes? Or would he drive by, oblivious?

Headlights appeared at last. Holly's captor stiffened. When the car drew to a halt nearby, Holly was hurled to the ground. Her captor crashed through the bushes, encumbered by a black-hooded slicker. Holly's heart sank; she'd be outnumbered now.

To her surprise, however, her attacker climbed into a station wagon, which made a U-turn and shot back down the driveway.

Still trembling, Holly limped back to Lyon House. All the downstairs lights were off except the hall spotlight. As she tiptoed by the praying hands statue, she remembered Aunt Prissy's warning not to touch it. Disaster had indeed followed—engineered by the old lady?

The next morning, Holly decided to play cat and mouse: pretend nothing had happened, and see if she could catch the enemy off guard.

Providing, of course, that her enemy was someone at Lyon House . . .

"Good morning," Aunt Prissy greeted the family. "Everyone sleep well?"

"Gloriously," said Carlotta. "Foggy nights remind me of Old Blighty. Mimi, dear, where did you go last night?"

"Me?" Mimi looked guilty.

"I peeked in your room around ten to see if you needed an extra blanket."

Mimi thrust out her lower lip. "I went out jogging."

Uneasily, Holly remembered seeing Mimi and the red-haired boy in a station wagon yesterday afternoon.

"Jogging on such a miserable evening?" Carlotta made a face. "That's the younger generation for you," she said to Aunt Prissy.

The old lady snorted. "I always enjoy jogging. No matter what the time—or the weather."

Jogging, Holly thought, indicated physical fitness, and strength for one's age. . .

"Give me wheels any time," said Tyler. "How are you today, Craig?"

"Not so hot." Craig's eyes were puffy, and his mouth was slack. "Orange juice and Bufferin should fix me up."

"What's the trouble?" Carlotta asked him.

"Flu, I guess." His hand trembled as he lifted a glass of juice.

"Have fun last night?" Tyler asked him, shooting a glance at Holly.

"Audrey had a few people over." Craig refused Saito's sausage omelets. "Just black coffee, thanks. Holly, would you tell Murray I'm sick?"

She nodded, wondering what time he'd returned last night.

"This breakfast is the last of the food I ordered," Carlotta announced. "You girls better market today."

"I can borrow a station wagon, Holly," said Mimi. "Pick you up after work?"

Holly nearly jumped out of her chair. "What about money?" she stalled.

"Today's pay day," said Mimi.

Aunt Prissy pulled a worn wallet from her tennis tote. "Who's treasurer?"

"Tyler's good at mathematics," Carlotta said.

"Don't forget the treasurer kicks in to the kitty, too," said Aunt Prissy.

"I'll take care of your share today, Tyler," Carlotta said hastily. "But maybe you'd better look for a job."

Tyler nodded. "Since Craig's staying home, I'll drive Holly to the *Gazette*."

"I'll take Mimi to her farm stand," Carlotta said. "I'd like to meet your boss, dear."

In his white Jaguar with black leather seats, Tyler seemed in such a mellow mood that Holly decided to question him.

"Were you here when my parents died?" she asked him.

He shook his head. "We were abroad."

Thus, with Craig at boarding school, and Aunt Prissy in New York, the only relative present had been the late Archibald Lyon.

"It must have been ghastly to lose both parents at once," Tyler said sympathetically. "I was really broken up when my Dad died. But at least Mimi and I have Mother."

Maybe Tyler Lyon was human after all! "Do you know how my parents died?" Holly asked.

"Just rumors." He slid his arm around the back of her car seat. "You're different from other girls, Holly. Sweet. Unspoiled." His hand gently squeezed her shoulder.

Was this a cousinly gesture of affection? Or a pass? Had this same hand worn a rubber glove last night?

"The family's afraid," Tyler continued seriously, "that if you dig up your past, you'll turn neurotic. Become like your mother. Why ruin *your* life, Holly? Wouldn't you be happier in Vermont?"

"Sure," she said honestly. "But first I want to find out the truth about my mother."

"In spite of the risks?" When she nodded, he removed his arm from her seat. "It's your funeral." His voice was light, but his choice of words made Holly wince.

At the *Gazette* office, Tyler introduced himself to Murray, then said, "I'd like to join Holly and Craig here."

"Doing what?"

"Well—as your administrative assistant? I took a great economics course at the University of Virginia."

Murray gazed at him. "This isn't a corporation. Everyone here is productive. Do you have any experience?"

"Extensive travel," said Tyler confidently. "I've even lived abroad. I could write a sophisticated travel column."

"That we don't need. How about selling ads?"

"Okay for starters, I guess," Tyler said.

"You'd work strictly on commission. All the adjoining towns are covered, but I've been thinking of hitting Locust Valley and Glen Cove."

"You mean I'd design ads for shopkeepers?" Tyler asked.

"Hardly," said Murray. "First you persuade them to *place* ads."

"Oh." Tyler hesitated. "How much will I make?"

"Figure on a month just to build up contacts. By mid-July, you may start selling. *If* you're lucky, and *if* you work like a dog."

Tyler looked outraged. "I need money now! How about an advance?"

Murray shook his head. "How do I know you'll bring in any business? Inexperienced people always start on commission. This is a small weekly paper, Tyler, not a training program."

"But Grandfather would never—"

"Mr. Lyon is dead," Murray growled, "and *I* am in charge of the *Gazette*."

Tyler's eyes narrowed. "Have you forgotten that we Lyons still own it legally?"

Murray shrugged.

"You'd better watch your step," Tyler snapped, and strode out.

Murray gave Holly several articles to type, told her he was going out, then asked, "Does Craig really have flu?"

Holly nodded. "He looked awful. Couldn't even eat breakfast."

To economize, Holly had brought a sandwich of leftover roast beef for lunch. She decided to do some research on her mother during lunch hour. Thompson Hospital could be a good clue to her mother's troubled past, but it wasn't listed in the Nassau or Suffolk County telephone directories. She phoned several hospitals, but none had heard of Thompson.

Later, Murray noticed the list. "What's that?" he asked.

"Research. I wrote a series on Vermont hospitals for my school paper. This is comparative information for a follow-up next fall. I did it on my lunch hour," she added hastily.

"Hospital series . . ." Murray looked thoughtful. "Good service to the community. Want to try it for the *Gazette*? You could start with rest homes and nursing homes. But your visits will have to be on weekends; I need you here during the week."

It hadn't occurred to Holly that Thompson might be a rest home. "Super!" she said. "My first professional assignment."

Murray handed her two pay envelopes, one for herself, the other for Craig. "You're doing a nice job, Holly. As long as you pull your weight, you won't find me too tough a boss."

Holly cashed her check, for two days' work, at the local bank. Then she met Mimi in the village parking lot.

"I've chosen the vegetables and fruit for the week." Mimi gestured at the rear of the station wagon. "Let's plan the dinner menus before we hit the supermarket for staples and meat."

"How come you know about budget food shopping?" Holly asked curiously.

"I've kept house," said Mimi with obvious pride. "I live off-campus with—with someone. We're always broke."

From her tone, Holly figured that Mimi's roommate was not another girl. Reminded again of the station wagon involved in last night's attack, she glanced uneasily at her cousin behind the wheel of this one. Mimi was fairly tall. Her hands looked strong. Was that red-bearded young man last night's accomplice?

"Do you have a special guy?" Holly asked, trying to sound casual.

Mimi stiffened. She peered angrily at Holly, then away. "The family thinks I live in a college dorm, so keep your mouth shut about that. And," she added ominously, "hands off my private life. If you want to survive the summer, that is."

57

Chapter 9

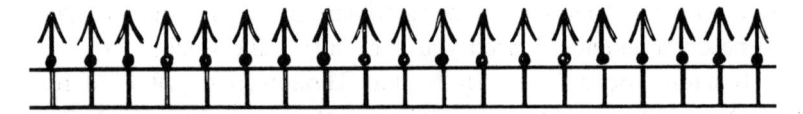

Although she still felt constantly wary, the following week passed without incident for Holly. There were no further threats or attacks, and the family reacted to budget meals with the eager curiosity of travelers in a foreign country.

One Saturday morning, Holly borrowed Peter Meade's car, arranging to pick him up later for a beach picnic. She drove first to a rest home near the village, where the cooperative head nurse gave her a tour and an interview.

No one there had heard of Thompson Hospital.

Several miles out of town, she found her next destination: THE MANOR, a turreted greystone mansion with a private golf course, an enormous swimming pool, four tennis courts and a putting green.

The white-coated director, Dr. Phipps, was type cast to television-perfection: handsome, deeply tanned, hair artfully greying at the temples. "I'm sorry," he told Holly in a deep voice that inspired confidence. "No press allowed here."

"The *Gazette*'s doing a survey of all the rest homes in the area," said Holly. "It's a community service to our readers."

"I'll explain, so you won't waste your time and ours." He led her into an opulent office. "This is an exclusive rest home. Our patients include famous professional men and powerful corporate executives. The women are top-drawer society. Social Register . . . jet set . . . trustees of country clubs and private schools. How would they feel if word leaked out that they'd been here?" His eyes probed hers. "We guarantee our patients absolute privacy."

The phone rang. While he answered it, Holly spotted several framed photographs of The Manor. One building was labeled Thompson House!

As soon as the doctor hung up, Holly asked eagerly, "Is Thompson House part of The Manor?"

He nodded. "It's a rehabilitation facility for alcoholics."

Holly's heart began to pound. Until now, the idea of her mother's being an alcoholic had never crossed her mind. "I think I had a relative here," she said.

Dr. Phipps looked quizzical. "Really? How convenient."

"About fourteen years ago." Holly persisted. "Can you look up her records for me?"

"We release medical information only to the patient's physician," said Dr. Phipps.

"She's dead, doctor," said Holly in a small voice.

"The same rule applies."

Holly thought of the letter with the doctor's signature torn off. "I don't know who her doctor was. But it would mean everything in the world to me to know why she was here."

"And it means 'everything in the world' to our patients to know that we guard their records," he said. "I'm sorry, Miss—er—Blake." He ushered her back to the reception hall.

As Holly passed the reception desk, she decided to make one more attempt. "How can I find out the name of a doctor who referred a patient here?" she asked the pink-uniformed receptionist, whose desk nameplate said "Sherry Francis."

"Whom did you have in mind?" Miss Francis asked.

"Julia Lyon Blake."

Miss Francis' eyes widened. "Any relation of Archibald Lyon?"

Holly nodded. "His cousin. Were you here when she was a patient at Thompson House?"

Miss Francis fiddled with some papers on her tidy desk. "I cannot give out that particular information. The name Lyon shook me up because everyone on the North Shore knows it. Good morning, Miss Blake," and she escorted Holly outside.

Holly figured that even if she mentioned Julia's being her mother, these people wouldn't cooperate without the required medical letter.

She drove off with her mind in a turmoil. She knew very little about alcoholism. She'd seen her friends get drunk or stoned at parties, but she'd never known an alcoholic. . . . Was Julia Lyon

Blake's alcoholism her disease? Was it the reason her mother was called "crazy" by the Blakes and "paranoid" and "strange" by the Lyons?

When she picked up Peter, he asked, "Why the long face?"

"A place called The Manor gave me the freeze treatment," she said.

Peter laughed. "Forget about it. Murray won't expect a story on The Manor."

They drove to a crowded public beach. Peter introduced Holly to a group sprawled around a picnic hamper, contributed a jug of cider, and spread towels for them. Basking in the sun, listening to music on a transistor radio, Holly really relaxed for the first time since she'd arrived at Laurel Cove. These boys and girls reminded her of the Vermont crowd.

The family was having cocktails on a veranda when Holly joined them later. She searched through an assortment of liquor bottles for the inexpensive sherry she'd purchased earlier last week.

"How about a daiquiri?" Craig held a silver shaker aloft.

"They're excellent," said Aunt Prissy.

"Just sherry, thanks," Holly said. "If I can find my bottle."

"My fault," said Craig. "Some friends dropped in this afternoon and drank it. I'll replace it Monday."

Slightly annoyed, Holly accepted a daiquiri as Tyler arrived on the porch, elegant in white ducks and a crimson blazer.

"Daiquiris!" he cried. "Perfect for a warm summer evening."

"I don't mean to be cheap, Tyler, but that rum's mine," said Craig. "You haven't bought any booze yet."

"Have a gin and tonic, dear," Carlotta suggested quickly. "The Gordon's mine."

Tyler pulled a gold money clip from his pocket. "Will ten bucks cover what I've had of your booze, Craig?"

Craig shrugged. "I guess so."

"Where'd you get the bankroll?" Mimi asked her brother.

"Sold my amethyst cuff links."

Carlotta gasped. "Oh, Tyler—*why*? They belonged to your father!"

"I need cash," Tyler said.

"What about the job interview I arranged at the Cove Bookshop?" Carlotta asked him.

"The owner wanted me to work Saturdays. I've signed up to crew at the Yacht Club on Saturdays."

"They don't pay," Aunt Prissy said.

"I'm a *yachtsman*!" Tyler cried. "I can't live in Laurel Cove all summer without racing!"

Mimi snorted. There was a tense silence, finally broken by Holly. "Does anybody know the name of my mother's doctor?"

"She probably used old Doc Wheelwright," said Aunt Prissy. "Archibald did, I know."

"Is he in the village?" Holly asked.

"In a manner of speaking," Aunt Prissy's tone was solemn. "He's buried there. Died three years ago." She threw back her head and cackled with laughter until the quadruple strand of pearls rattled and bounced on her bony chest.

Carlotta leaned forward with a concerned expression. "Do you need a doctor, Holly?"

"No. But I think I've found out what was wrong with my mother. I need her doctor's help to prove it." Her hand trembled as she poked a celery stalk into a silver bowl of dip.

"You mean a new-fangled name for her craziness?" Aunt Prissy asked.

Holly nodded. "Alcoholism."

Tyler burst out laughing. "Alcoholism? Your *mother*?"

"I found a hospital where she was a patient," Holly said. "Thompson House. It's at The Manor."

"Sure," said Craig. "Everyone knows the Manor."

Aunt Prissy started rocking back and forth in her wicker chair.

"Was she really in a drunk tank?" Tyler asked excitedly.

Holly took a deep breath. "My first night here, someone left an old letter in my room. It said that my mother should go to Thompson."

"Should go, or did go?" asked Mimi.

"Show us the letter," Carlotta suggested.

"It's gone," said Holly. "Someone took it back later, while I was on the phone." The blood rose slowly in her cheeks as the Lyons stared meaningfully at one another.

"Remember how Julia used to imagine that people were listening in on her telephone conversations?" said Aunt Prissy hoarsely. "Sometimes she even thought the phone was tapped."

Holly jumped to her feet. "I *held* that letter in my *hand*! It was wrapped around a yellow rose, the same color as—"

"Holly," said Craig, "your mother was only twenty-six when she died. Too young to be an alcoholic."

"And too pretty and intelligent," added Carlotta. "We all know she was neurotic, Holly, dear. The poor girl inherited that from your Cousin Archibald."

"No. From my aunt," said Aunt Prissy.

"What about the clause in Cousin Archibald's will, about nobody getting drunk in public?" Holly demanded. "Could he have been afraid I might inherit her alcoholism?"

Craig refilled her glass, then his own. "Did Dad's letter mention alcoholism?"

Holly shook her head.

"Then you're jumping to a crazy conclusion. No Lyon's ever been an alcoholic."

"Furthermore," added Tyler, "your mother's been dead for fourteen years."

"Let her rest in peace," Mimi said.

Holly took a deep swallow of her fresh drink. "All my life I've wanted to know what was wrong with her. At last I have the chance. Why won't anyone help me?" Her voice broke.

"Because you get too upset," said Carlotta. "You work yourself into a state, *exactly* as Julia used to do."

Aunt Prissy wagged a gnarled finger. "All Archibald's money will be useless to you if you turn out like Julia."

Rage finally exploded inside Holly. "You're all trying to make me think I'm crazy!" she cried. "You didn't expect any outside competition for the estate! But Archibald Lyon loved me, even though we never met. He told me so in that beautiful letter. He *wanted* me to spend the summer here!" She glared at each Lyon in turn. "So whoever's trying to scare me out of Lyon House can just forget it. I'm half a Vermonter, and we Yankees don't scare easily!"

Craig gripped Holly's shoulders. "Easy, sweetie. What's this about somebody trying to scare you?"

Holly suddenly longed to fling herself into his arms and pour out everything. But what if he was the enemy? "Whoever it is knows I'm not imagining it," she said, hoping with all her heart and soul that it wasn't Craig.

"Julia had fears like this before her severe spells." Aunt Prissy rocked until her wicker chair squeaked.

"But I'm *not* my *mother*!" Holly cried, shaking free of Craig. "I'm half my father, too! He was a sensible, predictable, Vermont school teacher—a *square*! Yet you all assume I'm irrational like my mother. How do you think that makes *me* feel?"

"Paranoid," said Tyler with a snicker.

"It's no joke!" Holly flung at him. "Somebody's trying to scare me into thinking I'm insane so I'll leave Lyon House!"

"Calm down!" Carlotta spoke sharply, then rose and put her arm around Holly. "You have a right to try for the estate, the same as everybody else. But Aunt Prissy does have a point: Your mother was prone to paranoia; sometimes she fantasized that weird people and things were after her. *We* don't think you have a mental problem, dear. But perhaps you've inherited just a little of this *tendency* from her."

Carlotta's tone was so sympathetic, her arm so reassuring, that Holly sat down again, slowly.

"We're all very fond of you," Carlotta continued. "We certainly don't want you to feel paranoid about *us*. But we must all trust one another. Doesn't that make sense, dear?"

She smiled warmly at Holly, who nodded reluctantly.

"Why not begin by showing us Archibald's letter?" Carlotta added. "I suspect the old codger wrote something puzzling, that scared you, but that one of us can easily explain."

At that moment, Saito announced dinner.

"Run up and get the letter first," Tyler suggested. "We'll wait."

Holly shook her head. She still felt she shouldn't show the letter to the family, in case one member was holding out on her. Later, if her antagonist turned out to be someone outside the family, she might reconsider.

After dinner, when Aunt Prissy asked Holly to fetch her needlepoint, Holly peeked curiously inside the old lady's closet. Stuffed between two dresses was a black, hooded slicker, and in a bureau drawer, she found a harmonica, a flute, and a stack of sheet music!

She was about to examine the music to see if "The Holly and the Ivy" was included when a voice said, "Miss?" and Saito slid out of the adjoining bathroom. "Miss Holly need help?" His expression was impassive.

"N-no," Holly stammered. "I—I was just getting some wool for Miss Lyon. Thanks anyway, Saito," and she fled.

Downstairs, as Aunt Prissy yanked the needlepoint from the bag, Holly stared at the former gym teacher's hands. Were they strong enough to shove a large boulder over a cliff? To overpower her? Or would her great-aunt need an accomplice?

"You look as if you've seen a ghost," the old lady observed. "Who's prowling around upstairs?"

"Just Saito." Holly tried to sound casual.

Aunt Prissy chuckled. "That one's *like* a ghost. Appears when you least expect him—sneaking around in those black slippers. But then again, maybe our ways seem strange to him, eh?" She shoved her needle into the canvas with such gusto that Holly murmured an excuse and quickly left the room.

Chapter 10

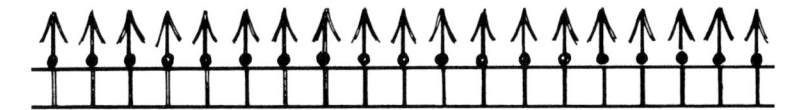

Monday morning at the office, Holly asked Peter who had taken over Dr. Wheelwright's practice after he died.

"His patients were absorbed by a group," Peter said. Then realizing that Holly had never seen an obituary of her mother, he brought her an old, bound volume of *Gazette* issues. Under the headline GAZETTE OWNER'S NIECE KILLED IN AUTO ACCIDENT, was the first photograph Holly had ever seen of her mother.

Dark hair sprang in short, saucy curls from Julia's oval face; her mother's large eyes and slim figure resembled Holly's own.

How could this enchanting looking girl be the same person Grandpa Blake called "crazy" and the Lyons "paranoid?"

There was a brief accompanying article, dated February 9, fourteen years before.

> Julia Lyon Blake, 26, cousin and ward of *Gazette* owner Archibald E. Lyon, and her husband, Jack, 29, were killed early this morning when their car plunged off a cliff at Lyon House.

Holly looked up at Peter. "They died on my sixth birthday," she said in a choked voice. He patted her hand awkwardly, then she continued reading:

> Funeral services will be held at the Laurel Cove Church on Monday at 10 a.m. for Mrs. Blake, and in Shelburne, Vermont, for Mr. Blake.
>
> One daughter, Holly, 6, survives in Shelburne.

Folded into the center of the large volume was another clipping from a Long Island daily paper, one section marked in red:

> According to a guest, Mrs. Blake left an engagement party in Laurel Cove at midnight, alone and inebriated.

65

Her concerned husband borrowed a car from another guest and returned to Lyon House, a mansion owned by Mrs. Blake's guardian, Archibald E. Lyon.

The chauffeur of the rented limousine told *Newsday*, "Mr. Blake had a real row with Mrs. Blake. She put four bottles of whiskey in the back seat of their Plymouth. Then she got in the car. She was going back to that party, no matter what he said. Mr. Blake jumped in beside her, and she took off down that icy driveway like a madwoman.

"Then I heard this God-awful crash."

Holly shuddered and put a hand over her eyes, picturing her intoxicated mother at the wheel, curls flying, eyes recklessly wild. Then a skid . . . a squeal of brakes . . . perhaps her father reaching desperately for the wheel . . . and the plunge, fifty feet down that cliff, to the Lyons' private beach.

According to the coroner, Mrs. Blake's blood alcohol level indicated 'driving while intoxicated.'

Nassau County records show that after she was arrested in January for drunken driving, her third such arrest in 6½ years, Mrs. Blake's license was suspended for three months.

She was rumored to have spent several weeks recently at The Manor, Laurel Cove's exclusive society rest home.

The clipping fell from Holly's fingers.

"You didn't know how they died?" Peter asked.

She shook her head. "Only that Grandpa called Mother a 'murderer,'" she said in a tight voice.

"Maybe she wasn't all to blame," he suggested. "Maybe your father was loaded, too."

"No!" cried Holly, understanding at last her grandfather's hatred for Julia. "Pa was a teetotaler, like his parents. So it *was* my mother's fault. *She* had to drive that night, even though she was drunk out of her mind, and didn't even have a driver's license! *She* had to take more booze back to that party! Grandpa was right, Peter!" Her voice broke and she buried her face in her hands. "My mother *did* murder my father!"

"Aren't you being too hard on her?" Peter asked gently.

Holly shook her head vehemently. "It's an eight-hour drive

from here to Shelburne. She didn't even think of staying sober for my sixth birthday. Her only child!"

"I doubt she *planned* to get drunk," he said.

"But she'd just spent several weeks at that beautiful Manor! She was nothing but a—a thoughtless, selfish, party girl!"

"Just because of one night?"

"That night tells the whole story! Oh, Peter—for years I've hoped and prayed that Grandpa somehow made a terrible mistake. That Mother *couldn't* have been as awful as he said. But now I understand. She should never have been a mother at all!"

"Cool it," said Peter sharply. "You're talking yourself into hating your own mother. That'll make *you* sick."

Holly stared incredulously at him. "How could you understand? With your normal, apple-pie parents? I'll bet there isn't even a hidden cartilage in your whole family closet!"

"My folks are human," he said quietly, "and so was your mother. Don't let yourself hate her, Holly."

"Stop lecturing me!" she shouted, as the door to another office flew open.

"Holly!" said Craig. "What the devil's the matter?"

Wordlessly, she pointed to the clipping. Craig scanned it, then reached down and gathered her into his arms.

With a strangled cry of relief, Holly burst into tears. "It was my birthday," she sobbed. "How *could* she?"

"I know." Craig stroked her hair with gentle fingers. "Dad did it to me once. Five guys—tickets to the Mets. We waited at Lyon House all afternoon, but he never showed."

"What happened?" Holly's voice was muffled against his chest.

"He went sailing with friends. Completely forgot about me. Told me later that he hated baseball."

"What?" blurted Peter.

"He hated baseball," Craig repeated.

"But Mr. Lyon dug baseball! He took me to six Mets games last summer."

Craig stiffened. "Back off!" he snapped. "No comments from the peanut gallery." He tipped up Holly's face and looked into

67

her tear-drenched eyes. "Wash your face, sweetie. I'll take you to the Club for lunch."

The Yacht Club veranda was cooled by a light sea breeze. They sipped gin-and-tonics without speaking. Holly watched the tanned, cheerful members greeting one another, eating lunch in genial groups, and striding down the smooth lawn to the dock, where launches ferried them to the immaculate yachts anchored in the harbor.

She began to calm down in this safe, sure world.

"Did you know that your parents eloped?" Craig suddenly asked her.

Astonished, she shook her head.

"Dad wouldn't give Julia permission to marry Jack." He hesitated. "You were born six months later."

Holly felt her cheeks flush. "So I'm a love child," she said bitterly. "But one Mother didn't want. She sure proved that later."

"Abortions weren't legal in those days," Craig reminded her. "Thank God. Or you wouldn't be here now." He laid his hand over hers. "Some of us draw parents who are losers," he continued. "We have to reject them, or they'll drag us down with them."

"You mean your father?" she asked.

He nodded. "The last time I ever saw Dad, we quarreled. That was nothing new, but all of a sudden I realized how much I hated him. For once, I quit trying to relate. I split for Spain the next day and never came back." He lit a cigarette. "Now Dad's thrown me one more curve ball through his will. Figured I couldn't handle a full-time job. But I'll show him." He blew out a long stream of smoke. "Dad was a mean s.o.b., but I'm tough, too."

"You knew my mother." said Holly. "Was she a party girl?"

He nodded. "And how! Parties were all she thought about."

"Your father must have known that by coming here I'd find out what she was like," said Holly.

Nodding again, Craig drummed his fingers on the table. "Dad hurt a hell of a lot of people. Your mother did, too. It's okay for us to resent them—they deserve it."

"Peter says I'll get sick if I hate my mother," Holly said.

"You'll get sick if you *don't*," said Craig. "Peter doesn't have a neurotic family. How could he understand?" When he squeezed her hand, a thrill tingled along her arm. "If you get upset about your mother again, don't go to Peter. Come to me instead. That's what relatives are for." After all, he *was* a third cousin once removed. Hardly a cousin at all!

The look he gave her was hardly cousinly, however, and Holly was about to confide in him about the cliff-top attack when a friend of his joined them for lunch. Holly had no further chance for personal conversation.

That afternoon, Murray suggested she write an article about a small hospital twenty miles from Laurel Cove. Grateful to be diverted from painful thoughts about her mother, Holly borrowed the *Gazette* car, inspected the hospital, and interviewed several staff members. Afterward, in a nearby drugstore, she carried a Coke to an old-fashioned, high-backed booth and settled down to check over her notes.

A young male voice ordered three iced teas. A pair of familiar greenish cowboy boots passed Holly's table, and she looked up to see Mimi's boyfriend. He swung into the booth ahead of hers.

Moments later, voices rose clearly over the high partition.

"It'll work out," a young man said.

"What'll we do if someone finds out?" a female voice said with a British accent.

"No one will, old girl." A male voice, also with a British accent.

"Certainly not from us." The woman again. "After all, we're not normally chatty types." Her laugh sounded sinister.

"We didn't see anybody we knew," said Mimi's boyfriend.

Holly heard the rustle of bills.

"On the nose," said the British man.

As they got up to leave, Holly ducked down out of sight below her table. For the woman, wearing a sleeveless dress and sandals, was Su Chen! And the man in a sports shirt, clapping Mimi's boyfriend jovially on the back, was Saito!

"Keep it quiet," said the boy with the red hair and beard.

Pretending to search for something on the floor, Holly watched their feet go by her booth.

"Otherwise," Mimi's boyfriend was saying, "all our plans will be down the drain."

Chapter 11

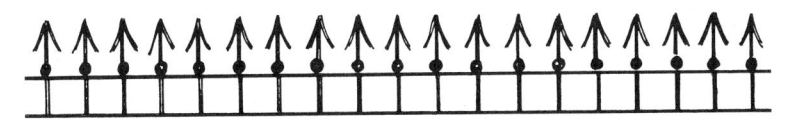

On July Fourth weekend, the Lyons gave a beach party.

They had asked Holly how her hometown friends entertained on a low budget, and she had described a typical Vermont cookout. Carlotta took charge of the arrangements, assessing each family member twenty-five dollars. Mimi, however, said it was a waste of money and declared that she wouldn't attend.

The morning of the party, Murray asked Holly to cover two parades and a girls' softball game. Consequently, she was away from Lyon House most of the day.

When she arrived on the private beach at dusk, she saw at once that this "informal cookout," as Carlotta had worded the invitations, didn't resemble a typical Shelburne party. Card tables were set up as a buffet, with formal china and silver. Back home everyone wore old clothes, but tonight Holly felt awkward in her jeans and sneakers—all eighty guests were fashionably dressed for evening.

Instead of the agreed-upon pitchers of beer and 7-up, Tyler stood behind a portable bar, making cocktails to order. Saito and Su Chen circulated through the crowd, bearing silver platters arranged with raw vegetables.

"Thanks." Holly selected a zucchini round heaped with Brie cheese. She'd been tempted, since that June afternoon in the Glen Cove drugstore, to confront Saito and Su Chen about their fluent English, but fear made her silent.

Down the beach, she recognized a steward from the Yacht Club tending an enormous hibachi covered with foil-wrapped corn and potatoes. Nearby, a table held piles of hot dogs, each neatly impaled on a long stick; toasted rolls; and a half dozen silver bowls of assorted condiments.

She spotted Craig. Audrey Woodward was at his elbow, exotic

in a silver-patterned jumpsuit. Holly noted with grim satisfaction that Audrey lurched whenever the high heels of her sandals sank into the sand.

Aunt Prissy was perched on a canvas director's chair in lace hostess pajamas, babbling excitedly to several contemporaries.

Holly didn't recognize most of the guests. She smiled tentatively at one or two, but they glanced at her, then quickly away. Feeling rebuffed, she contemplated sneaking up to her room.

"Wish you were at the Hamburg Nook?" Peter Meade asked.

"I didn't know you were coming!" Holly cried.

Appropriately dressed in red slacks and a plaid sports jacket, he gestured with a camera. "Mrs. Lyon invited me to cover the bash." He looked around at the crowd. "Mr. Lyon gave a beach party last Fourth of July. He didn't invite these society types, though."

"Who came?"

"Mostly the gang you've met at the Hamburg Nook. Maybe we weren't in the right clubs, but we sure had more laughs."

"I wish you could see our Vermont cookouts," said Holly wistfully. "Everyone is so *friendly* up home."

He peered quizzically at her through his squarish, tortoise-shell glasses. "North Shore society giving you the deep freeze tonight?"

Holly nodded.

"They'd smother you with attention if they knew you might inherit this spread. Say—didn't the Lyons clue you about clothes?"

"No." Holly glanced up the steep cliff. The setting sun turned the yellow rose bush a deep, glowing gold. She started to tremble.

"Hey, little girl!" Peter wrapped a long arm around her shoulders. "You're shivering. How about a drink?"

Holly had avoided being alone with Peter since their argument about her mother. But he was nice, and with Audrey monopolizing Craig this evening, she could use an escort. He stopped to photograph someone; Holly continued alone to the bar.

"Two more martinis. Doubles," Craig told Tyler.

Tyler whistled. "This'll be your fourth. Getting loaded before we toast the franks?"

Craig laughed. "Who's loaded?"

"You'll violate Grandfather's will if you get intoxicated in public," Tyler quoted the document.

"Correction. I am not in a public *place*." Craig pointed dramatically to the high water mark, several yards below on the beach. "I'm on Lyon House property."

"One step over that mark, and you could be out of the running." Tyler smiled wolfishly. "Not that I'd turn you in. But we don't know who the trustees of the estate are."

"Carrot, sir?" Saito slid into view from behind Craig, his white jacket conspicuous in the deepening dusk. Had Saito overheard? Would those black eyes be on the alert for Craig to step across the water line? To whom would he report later?

Carlotta approached. "Are you the boy from the *Gazette*?" she asked Peter, who nodded. "The guests are going to toast their own frankfurters. It's a quaint Vermont custom called hot-dogs-on-a-stick. So, if you'll just come this way. . . ."

As Peter grabbed Holly's hand, Carlotta whirled around. "Holly, dear! You didn't change for the party!"

"I'm sorry," Holly mumbled. "We always wear jeans."

"Run up and hop into something pretty."

"Carlotta!" Audrey called from beside the hibachi. "We'll be ready for the salad any minute."

"Where's Mimi?" Carlotta's green eyes searched the crowd.

"Is she coming after all?" Holly asked.

"She'd better," snapped Carlotta. "I invited all sorts of suitable young men for her." She shrugged impatiently and called to Audrey, "Holly's going up for the salad now. Saito made it in the glass punch bowl, so there's plenty."

As Holly passed Aunt Prissy, the old lady put out a be-ringed hand. "Planning to change up at the house?" she asked gruffly.

Holly nodded, uncomfortably recalling the slicker that she'd seen next to tonight's outfit in her great-aunt's closet.

"I noticed you haven't any real jewelry," Aunt Prissy said suddenly and unsnapped a beautiful gold link bracelet. "This belonged to your mother."

The heavy bracelet fitted Holly's slim wrist perfectly. Overwhelmed by the unexpected gesture, she said, "Thank you so much. I've never had anything of Mother's before." She bent and kissed the old lady's wrinkled cheek.

"I removed it from her room after she died," Aunt Prissy announced. "Along with the ivory dresser set."

"Did you give me those brushes the night I arrived?" Holly asked.

When Aunt Prissy nodded, Holly wondered uneasily if the old lady had also left the letter from Julia's doctor.

"I sense trouble tonight," Aunt Prissy rasped, her eyes shining oddly. "Be careful. One tragedy in your family was enough."

Holly froze. She wasn't drunk, as her mother had been the night she'd died. What did Aunt Prissy mean?

She started up to the house, shaken by the old lady's warning. In addition, this mockery of a simple Vermont cookout made her deeply homesick for Shelburne. How could she last the whole summer here? But, she reminded herself, she'd survived one month already, and her reasons for staying still outweighed those for leaving.

Darkness had fallen when Holly left the house, now wearing dressy slacks and an embroidered white top and carrying the enormous cut glass bowl of salad. When she reached the cliffs, she set it down and rubbed her aching arms. Her new gold bracelet made her feel close to her mother again.

She peered over the dark precipice. Kerosene torches on tall poles revealed the guests seated and eating on folding chairs or blankets, plates of food balanced on their knees. Two white coats gleamed in the semi-darkness, as Saito and Su Chen glided through the crowd with trays of wine glasses.

The Beautiful People, Holly thought wryly. She used to assume that being rich meant that cares would automatically vanish. But she was learning this summer that the Beautiful People had plenty of problems, too.

She could see Peter easing away from the lighted area, carrying food to someone down the beach. At that moment, a speedboat swung inland, and Holly recognized Mimi in its powerful searchlight.

Peter had never mentioned that he knew Mimi!

What was going on? Was Peter in with Mimi's redheaded boy friend, and Saito and Su Chen? Or did Mimi and Peter have something going?

As Holly headed down the steps, her bare arms wrapped around the heavy salad bowl, the speedboat swung away from the beach. The stairs were dark, and she hoped she wouldn't trip.

Two seagulls cried to one another. Something rustled in the bushes. She thought of Aunt Prissy's warning and halted. Even the night air pulsated with sudden, ominous danger.

"Stop it!" she told herself grimly. Who would pull some stunt during a big party?

But she knew that she was vulnerable. What if somebody chose this moment to shove a boulder down this staircase?

She heard a soft moan. Was it another seagull? Or a human? She listened, every nerve alert.

Silence now. No further rustles, and the seagulls were still.

"Don't become paranoid like your mother!" she admonished herself.

Then, with the sinking sensation that follows dread premonitions coming true, she heard the soft moans of a harmonica. The tune was chillingly familiar:

> *The Holly and the Ivy . . .*
> *When they are both full-grown . . .*

Her heart leaped into her throat. Had Aunt Prissy tucked her harmonica in a pocket of that lace pantsuit? If so, why the touching gift of the bracelet?

> *Of all the trees that are in the wood,*
> *The Holly stands alone . . .*

As the song throbbed to a close, Holly figured that the harmonica player must be in the beach house. Only a few feet away.

Who was watching her through that nearby black window? What would happen next?

She set the salad bowl down, and turned to run up the stairs. Then she heard a whimper from well below the beach house. Or was night playing tricks on her hearing?

She crouched, straining to see in the darkness. A frog croaked. Holly jumped. Had *that* been the whimper?

Another croak from the middle of the cliff.

Frogs don't play harmonicas.

Now she heard a moan. This was no animal. It was human, and in pain.

Down on the beach she could hear the muted sounds of the party: clinking silverware, people chatting, an occasional laugh.

Then she heard a weak but distinct call for help.

Holly waited no longer. Glancing nervously at the window, she felt her way down the stairs as fast as she could in the dark.

A flickering torch at the foot of the final staircase faintly illumined something in the sand.

Holly paused. What if this were a trick?

Instinct told her that it was not, and she headed for a shadow on the sand, her heart pounding in her ears, her palms moist from terror.

Then she looked aghast at the crumpled figure of Aunt Prissy, lying face down in the sand.

Chapter 12

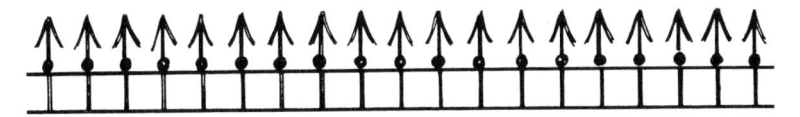

"Help!" screamed Holly, "Help, somebody, please! Aunt Prissy's hurt!"

Arriving first, Saito felt Aunt Prissy's pulse, as Peter raced up the beach from the opposite direction, then on up to the house to phone an ambulance.

Craig caught Holly in his arms. "Thank God, *you're* not hurt."

"Someone's hiding in the beach house," she gasped.

Craig took the stairs two at a time. "Empty," he called. "How is Aunt Prissy, Saito?"

"Doctor here?" Saito asked, still on his knees beside the inert old lady. "Need doctor fast."

Even in this crisis, Holly noticed that he used pidgin English, and that Craig carefully articulated: "No doctor at party. We call ambulance. To go hospital."

"Stand back, please," Carlotta's tone was authoritative as guests crowded around Aunt Prissy. "What happened, Holly?"

"She was mugged, by someone in the beach house."

"He's gone," Craig announced.

Carlotta strode upstairs for a fruitless search of the small building. A few minutes later, she and Craig accompanied the still-unconscious Aunt Prissy to the hospital by ambulance. The guests quickly made excuses to depart, but Peter stayed to help cart debris up the long hill.

"What a drag!" complained Tyler angrily. "Our one party of the season, spoiled by that idiotic old fool losing her balance."

"Isn't she pretty old to navigate these stairs without help?" Peter asked.

"Aunt Prissy's still very athletic," said Holly. "Comes down here every day for a swim."

Saito and Su Chen shuffled by, carrying the heavily laden bar cart.

"Let's wrestle this big table up," Peter suggested to Tyler.

Working alone on the beach, Holly suddenly noticed that her mother's bracelet was gone. It had been on her wrist when she'd started down the cliff with the salad bowl, so she headed for the staircase with a flashlight.

Once again, the evening was hushed.

Halfway up the stairs, her flashlight revealed a hank of yarn caught in a bush. Smiling slightly, she recalled that Aunt Prissy had brought her needlepoint even to the dimly lit party.

Next, her light picked out a long strand of transparent nylon fishing line. Curious, she followed it a couple of feet along the cliffside, to where it was knotted to the trunk of a sturdy beach-plum. More fishing line was knotted to a bush on the other side of the staircase. Holly brought the two ends together. The original piece had been secured about six inches above the step.

Designed for somebody to trip over!

She was wondering with disgust who at Lyon House would want to harm old Aunt Prissy when the truth struck her. Everyone knew that Holly was about to descend these stairs in the dark, carrying a glass salad bowl too huge to see over. . . .

"You alone, miss?" His voice came from the top of the stairs.

Holly's mouth grew dry with fear. "I'm looking for my gold bracelet, Saito." Her voice cracked and she felt a chill run down her body.

"We help." He ran lightly down the steps, Su Chen close behind.

They could easily overpower her. Should she run for it down the beach?

"Harbor looks great with the moon out." Peter's voice floated down the hill.

"But no guests to see it," said Tyler morosely.

"Hi, guys!" Holly called hysterically. "Anybody see a gold bracelet?"

"Didn't know you owned one." Tyler's voice sounded mercifully near now.

"Aunt Prissy gave it to me tonight," Holly said.

Peter spotted the bracelet, half-buried in the sand. He asked

Holly in low tones, "What did you see on those stairs just now?"

"Nothing," said Holly uneasily, remembering his furtive rendezvous with Mimi.

"Who are you protecting?" His face was tense.

"Miss lose sweater, too?" Materializing from the shadows, Saito handed Holly a shawl that she recognized as Mimi's.

"What did you see on those stairs?" Peter persisted.

"I'm tired, Peter," said Holly quickly, wondering if he played the harmonica. "I think I'll head up to bed."

He shrugged. "When you're ready to talk, I'll be waiting."

The next morning at breakfast, Craig told Holly that Aunt Prissy had suffered a concussion and strained hip. "I'm surprised that she stumbled," he said. "She knows that staircase as well as one of her needlepoint patterns." He gazed quizzically at Holly. "By the way, sweetie, why such terror when you screamed last night?"

They were alone in the gloomy dining room. Holly watched a small black fly beat against a window screen. It was desperate to escape and return to its bright world outside, but trapped by a mesh limitation it could never fathom. Flies were incapable of asking for help, but Holly was a human being with a brain. She knew she'd reached the breaking point.

"Aunt Prissy didn't stumble," she said. "She tripped. Over a transparent fishing line knotted above the steps."

"Who the devil would want to trip a harmless old lady?" Craig asked angrily.

"I think it was meant for me," said Holly in a small voice.

"*You*?" His eyes widened. "Carrying that glass bowl? My God, Holly. What makes you think so?"

Saito glided through the swinging door with a pot of coffee.

"Let's go for a drive," Craig suggested.

He drove slowly while Holly debated with herself about confiding in him. Everyone at Lyon House was on her suspect list. Although her heart assured her that Craig was innocent, she needed proof.

"Do you play the harmonica?" she asked finally.

He shook his head.

"Do you—do you know how to whistle?"

"Nope. Tin ear. Can't even carry a tune. Why?"

Unburdening herself brought overwhelming relief. She omitted only the contents of Archibald's letter.

When she finished, Craig said, "I heard Carlotta call to you about the salad! Anyone could have sneaked up the stairs, fixed the line, and rejoined the party without being noticed."

Holly nodded. "I wish I knew who."

"So do I," he said grimly, guiding the car into a deserted parking lot. He slid his arm around the back of her seat. "If anything happened to you . . ." His voice trailed off. "Think you should leave Lyon House? Go back to Vermont?"

Holly's heart quickened at the tender expression in his eyes. "No way. Grandpa wants me to stick to my decision to stay here, and I can't afford a hotel."

"I can't stake you to one." He gathered her into her arms, tucking her head into the curve of his neck. "From now on, promise you'll be careful? No more wandering alone at night—*anywhere*." He ran a finger lightly along her jaw. "You mean so much to me . . ." he said, then tipped her chin up and kissed her lightly.

That night, Craig installed a heavy bolt on Holly's bedroom door. He also started taking her out.

He taught her to play backgammon over stingers at the Yacht Club. They hit his favorite bars in various North Shore villages. They dropped in on his friends; those who lived on estates had an attitude of entitlement similar to that of the Lyons. This feeling that they deserved special privileges, Holly decided, evolved from generations of affluent living.

Holly was swept off her feet. She'd never before gone out with a rich man; in fact, she often paid her own way on dates at college, but Craig wouldn't hear of this. His cavalier attitude made her feel delightfully old-fashioned and feminine.

He was a fascinating conversationalist, well read in many areas, and eloquent about his extensive travels. Encouraging about her writing, he offered constructive criticism about her articles.

Their sudden closeness did not go unnoticed by the family.

On Thursday, after work, Holly was sweeping the long back porch when Tyler strolled out, carrying a goblet of iced tea. "Isn't it Craig's turn for the veranda this week?"

Holly nodded. "He's over there washing his Porsche. I don't mind."

"Of course not, since he's the heir apparent and you're the mystery guest. Shrewd." Tyler perched on a glider. "Watch it, Holly. Audrey Woodward doesn't dig competition. She's out of town this week, but she'll fight back. She's always assumed she would eventually marry Craig."

"Who's talking marriage?" Holly felt a blush creep over her cheeks.

Tyler snickered. "Craig may play for the summer, but once that will is read, he'll drop you like a hot potato. Unless you win."

"Do you have a job yet?" Holly snapped, glancing at his white yachting shorts and topsiders.

Now it was Tyler's turn to look embarrassed. "I'm following up on several good leads. But more important, the boat I'm racing is doing well. Grandfather would be proud of me. I'm sure his trustees will feel that my sailing is. . . ." He paused and spoke pompously, in the language of the will, "A first-class indication of how I'd handle the estate."

Holly wasn't so sure, remembering that Archibald had sold his own yacht. "As long as you ante up for groceries," she said.

His lip curled. "I'm paying my way." His gaze flicked over his wrist, where a simple watch replaced his gold Patek Philippe. "Speaking of payment, how about your share of the booze for the party?"

"I've told you: I agreed to beer and soda," she said.

"Your pal Peter had a Chivas Regal and soda, and he wasn't even a guest."

"Dun your mother. She invited him," Holly said and marched off the porch to join Craig.

The next morning at breakfast, Holly and Mimi were making out their Friday supermarket list. The novelty of "truck driver dining," as Tyler termed it, had worn off for the family, and the girls were having trouble thinking up thrifty menus that wouldn't trigger complaints.

Menu planning had brought the girls together, but Mimi's clandestine friendships with Peter and the red-headed boy made

81

Holly feel a little uncomfortable with her cousin.

"How about pork chops?" Holly suggested. "They're on special."

Mimi made a face.

"I thought you liked them. Remember your recipe for frying them with green peppers and—"

"Please." Mimi held up her hand. She looked ill in the bleak dining room light.

"You okay?" Holly asked.

Mimi shook her head. "Let's not discuss food right now."

The phone rang. "Miss Woodward for you, sir," Saito called to Craig, who was in the library.

Holly could clearly hear Craig say, "Hi, honey—" before his voice dropped to a murmur. Her throat closed over her scrambled eggs. Now that Audrey was back, would Craig drop her?

"Someone invited me to the Yacht Club dance next weekend," Craig announced a few moments later. "But I told her I already have a date. Will you go with me, Holly?"

The gloomy room seemed to brighten.

When he went into the butler's pantry, Mimi whispered, "You're better for him than that snob, Audrey."

"Thanks." Holly's eyes shone. She wanted to share her joy with everyone, including mysterious Mimi. "Can I do anything for you? Call your boss and say you're sick?"

As Craig returned, Mimi said quickly, "I feel fine."

At noon, Craig went with Carlotta to see Aunt Prissy in the hospital. An hour later, Murray asked for him: "He's due at Village Hall at one o'clock. Told him yesterday."

Aware of Craig's relaxed time sense, Holly said, "I'm going for lunch. Want me to check for you?"

He nodded. "It's an important hearing. I want complete coverage."

Craig wasn't at Village Hall. The hearing, on a proposed condominium in a two-acre zoned area, had just begun, so Holly started taking notes.

Almost at once, she knew she was out of her depth.

She didn't know the names of the angry citizens who were strongly opposed to the condominium. Their speeches were peppered with unfamiliar terms and names, and she didn't know any of the officials. Sketching a map, she numbered each person's chair, praying that Craig would arrive soon.

But he didn't appear, and the debate grew increasingly heated. Holly's pencil flew, her head spun, her hand tired, but she stayed because Murray had stressed "complete coverage."

When she got back to the *Gazette* at two-thirty, neither Murray nor Craig was there. Worried, she typed her notes into a rough draft of an article.

Had Aunt Prissy taken a turn for the worse? Surely Craig would call her if there was a crisis.

Murray phoned at three. When he asked about the hearing, she said quickly, "Don't worry. The other line's ringing," and disconnected her boss.

At three-thirty, Craig finally appeared. "My God!" he cried. "The hearing! I completely forgot!" He clapped a hand to his forehead. "Going to the hospital wiped me out."

"How's Aunt Prissy?" Holly asked.

"Off the danger list, but she'll be bedridden for a while." He picked up her notes and scanned them. "This looks terrific. I'll give you the missing names."

They heard Murray's voice on the staircase. "If Craig forgot that hearing, I'll *fire* him!"

Craig turned pale. "I haven't been late to work all week."

"Take the article," Holly whispered.

He shook his head. "Not ethical."

"It wasn't your fault Aunt Prissy got sick," Holly whispered urgently. "Murray's too hard on you sometimes. Rewrite this. He'll never have to know I took the notes!"

Chapter 13

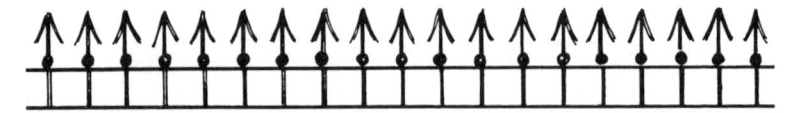

When Murray praised Craig for "his" article, Holly daydreamed about becoming a renowned man-woman journalism team. Her euphoria lasted until dinner time, when Tyler made a face at the baked macaroni and cheese. "No thanks, Saito. I'll just have salad." He turned to Carlotta. "Aren't you glad we ordered the steak and lobster tails at the Club?"

She nodded, refusing the macaroni with a delicate shudder. "Luncheon took too long, though. My partner for the qualifying round was annoyed. She'd hired a golf cart."

Holly stared at Craig. "I thought you visited Aunt Prissy."

"We did," said Carlotta. "The old dear's already demanding a wheelchair. But the nurses let us stay for only ten minutes."

Appalled, Holly thought of *her* afternoon: frantic note taking, skipping lunch, typing her notes—all to save Craig's job.

And *he'd* been enjoying a long gourmet luncheon!

Later, Craig said, "Forgive me, Holly? I'm not used to a full-time job. I'll need time to adjust. You've given me another chance."

The intimate look and the sincere tone appeased her. After all, Craig had helped with *her* articles recently. She'd never before liked a man this much, and real love was supposed to be for worse as well as for better . . .

The next day, Craig had lunch at his desk and worked straight through the afternoon.

Holly dressed for the Yacht Club dance in a frosted pink gown, piling her hair high on top of her head. Her mother's gold bracelet was her only jewelry.

Tyler shook his head in amazement when he saw her. "You'll be the most gorgeous girl at the Club!" In his formal yacht captain's outfit with the gold buttons and braid, he looked to her like a musical comedy performer. "I think we should level about something," he continued. "I had a talk with Mom today. I've been treating you the way I treat Mimi. It's not fair, Holly. You're a nice girl."

Was his tone sincere? Or did he have a sinister plan for tonight? "I'm willing to be friends," she said cautiously. "After all, we're cousins." But, nonetheless, she'd keep her eyes and ears open.

Craig looked elegant in a perfectly fitting tuxedo—a dream escort.

The Yacht Club's central hall, with its rows of nautical flags and glass cases of silver trophies, had been cleared for dancing to an orchestra. Another room held a buffet at least twenty feet long, and a porch contained tables set for eight.

Holly spotted Carlotta, the vivacious center of an older group. Tyler was having cocktails with a college-age crowd.

"Craig, darling," Audrey was wearing a white silk gown cut low down the back. Ropes of gold festooned her neck and arms. "I'd like you to meet Dr. Bud Phipps. Bud, this is Craig Lyon."

"Awfully glad to see you."

Holly recognized the doctor from The Manor, his tan accentuated by a white dinner jacket.

Dr. Phipps pumped Craig's hand. "Sailed a couple of times with your Dad. Wonderful fellow."

"Holly Blake, doctor," Craig said.

"Pleasure, Holly." He grasped her hand. "Haven't we met before? You in my niece's class at Vassar?"

She shook her head. "I met you last month at The Manor. On a *Gazette* assignment."

"Oh, yes," his smile vanished. "We have a strict policy of no publicity," he said to Craig. "Your Dad always respected it."

"I also asked about a former patient," Holly reminded him.

"Same deal."

"Holly's mother was my second cousin," Craig said.

"*Really*? Holly, why the devil didn't you say so? Glad to cooperate when we know somebody. Drop around next week."

Craig led her to a group of his friends, all in their late twenties. Conversation centered on the stock market, sailing, and small children.

First Holly felt shy, then slighted. Audrey was mentioned several times; these people obviously thought of Craig and Audrey as a couple. When Craig became engrossed in a technical discussion about sailboat racing, the party smile grew stiff on Holly's face. She'd fantasized a lot about tonight. Now she was being totally ignored.

The orchestra struck up a rock number. Holly tapped her foot eagerly, but nobody in this group seemed interested. Their voices rose over the music as they ordered another round of drinks from a steward.

"Want to dance?" she asked Craig.

He looked surprised. "To this?"

She nodded. A friend laughed, "Go ahead, fella. We've been ignoring your date."

They stood apart on the dance floor. Craig was stiff and self-conscious, but Holly gave herself completely to the compelling beat.

When the number ended, she grinned happily up at him, "Wasn't that super?"

He shook his head. "Never learned that stuff."

"Want me to teach you?" She caught his hand as another song started, one with a really wild rhythm, and her hips and feet automatically obeyed.

"Hey!" Craig called over the noise. "Let's go. Our drinks have come."

"Please wait!" Holly was so involved in the music that she continued to dance alone. Craig's face grew dark with embarrassment.

Tyler tapped Craig on the shoulder. "May I?" He started gyrating expertly with Holly. They danced two more numbers, then the band took a break and Tyler excused himself.

Winded and warm, Holly stepped out on the back porch to cool off. Suddenly, beyond a bushy evergreen growing in a nearby tub, she heard familiar voices.

"Don't like Phipps," said Craig.

"I'm twenty-five," said Audrey. ". . . date like a casual teenager any more."

Holly listened intently.

"In his forties! . . . old enough to be your father!" said Craig.

"*Very* attractive," she said. ". . . established doctor."

Craig uttered an exclamation. Ice cubes rattled.

"Bud wants to marry me," Audrey said in a provocative tone. Craig laughed shortly. "I'm broke."

"My trust fund," she said.

"I'm not for sale."

"Noble. . . ."

"I'll work," he said. "Same as now."

Audrey snickered. ". . . *Gazette* wages? . . . dreary apartment . . . no travel . . . clubs . . . decent cars . . . designer clothes . . . beat your brains out, just to get by. . . ."

"Sounds pretty grim," he said.

Holly thought of Tyler's warning that Craig would drop Holly "like a hot potato" if she didn't win the estate. She edged closer to the tree, determined to find out where she really stood with Craig Lyon.

Audrey spoke again, "Going to the Garden Club Ball next weekend?"

"Tickets are two hundred bucks."

"That's just the penny-pinching I'm talking about!" she cried. "Darling, our crowd assumes that we'll all have the same life style when we get married. We *deserve* it. Nobody gives a damn whose money it is."

"What about self-respect?" he asked.

"That comes from passing our values on to our children," she said.

Holly winced, as Craig murmured something too low for her to hear.

"Can't your family persuade her to return to Vermont?" Audrey asked.

Holly stiffened.

"She won't go," said Craig, "Anyway, she has the same right to try for the estate as the rest of us."

"Not true!" said Audrey. "She's an interloper! She'll *never* belong in Laurel Cove!"

Wicker squeaked as Craig jumped up and strode to the porch railing. Audrey followed him, and Holly shrank back behind the evergreen.

"I need a refill, Craig. I'll sign this time."

"No need. I can still afford to buy a lady a drink." Craig reached into his back trouser pocket. "While we wait, want a splash of Jack Daniels?"

He drew out a slim flask and held it aloft. Silver gleamed in the glare of his cigarette lighter. A fiddle tuned up indoors, and suddenly a vivid memory exploded in Holly's brain . . .

It was fourteen years ago. Holly and her mother were sitting on the sidelines at a Vermont barn dance.

Holly's father came across the floor, carrying three cups of strawberry punch. "Please try a square with me, Julia?" he asked.

Holly's mother shook her head. "You know I'd rather not, Jack."

"But you *can*, Mommy," said Holly. "You've done it at home with me."

"Has she?" Her pa's usually serious face broke into a pleased grin. "Come then, Julia." He held out his hand.

Julia shook her head. "Holly, I told you not to tell anyone!"

"What's the matter, Mommy?" Holly felt sorry for her father. He looked so eager, and she'd heard her parents fighting lately. Maybe if they danced, they'd love each other again. "Pa will help you."

Still Julia shook her head.

"Oh, Mommy!" Holly's childish voice rose. "You weren't afraid last week when you drank that red stuff in your bedroom."

As her mother's face darkened with embarrassment, Holly realized that several people nearby were snickering.

"Shut up!" Julia called out to her daughter, then looked up at her husband. "I'd make a fool of myself. Your friends don't like me as it is, and I hate to be laughed at. You *know* that, Jack."

"All I know is, you won't make the effort any more," Jack said quietly, then turned and went off to dance with somebody else.

Holly saw that her mother's eyes were glistening with tears. She stuck out her small hand to comfort her, but a strange man walked up to them, leaned over, and whispered something in Julia's ear.

Julia smiled up at him, the radiant smile that the now-grown

Holly had forgotten until she saw her mother's picture in the *Gazette*. Then Julia nodded and slipped outdoors with the man.

Holly followed. She crouched behind the huge barn door, watching her mother swallow greedily from a flat glass bottle.

"Thanks." Julia wiped her mouth with the back of her hand. "My daughter embarrassed me so much I really needed that."

The man laughed intimately. "You're too young and pretty to be buried up here."

"Don't I know it!" Julia snatched the bottle again and swallowed deeply. "Sometimes I wish I wasn't either a wife *or* a mother!"

Holly cringed behind the rough, bulky door. Did Mommy *really* mean she wished she'd never married Pa? Or was she just sorry that Holly had been born? Was it because Holly said naughty things, like just now about her dancing in secret?

As the pair passed the bottle back and forth, Holly's tension mounted. Their conversation was too low for her to follow, but she knew even at age six that what these grownups were doing was wrong. Otherwise why hide outdoors like this, from Pa and everyone else?

When the bottle was empty, her mother went back inside. She marched up to Holly's father and pulled him into a square right in the middle of the room. At first, Holly was proud of her mother, surely the most beautiful woman there. Brown eyes flashing, cheeks rosy, Julia tapped her foot smartly during the musical introduction, her circle skirt whirling high around her shapely legs.

But then the dance began. In the middle of a simple do-si-do, Julia tripped, fell flat on her face, and burst into hysterical laughter. She started sobbing and had to be carried out of the barn by Holly's scarlet-faced father.

In the excitement, Holly had been completely forgotten by her parents.

The next day, Julia was ill with one of her "migraine headaches." Several days after that, Julia and Jack Blake left Vermont, never to see their daughter again. . . .

"Holly didn't grow up at Lyon House," Audrey's voice jerked Holly back to reality. "*You* did. Just because you quarreled with your father doesn't mean you have to hand over the works to some little country . . . leech!''

As Craig swallowed greedily, Holly darted forward and knocked the flask from his hand. Audrey squealed as the whiskey spread in a vicious brown stain down her white silk gown.

"Holly!" Craig barked.

"My new Halston!" Audrey screamed. "She's crazy, like her mother!"

"I am not!" Holly cried. "But it's because of my mother that I—''

"Cool it!" Tyler's strong fingers grasped Holly's arm. "People are staring," he said, as she tried to finish her sentence.

"I'll have to change," Audrey told Craig.

"Audrey—our deepest apologies," Tyler said, hauling Holly off the porch. "Now you've done it," he snapped. "I told you not to tangle with Audrey. She'll ruin us. The Woodwards rule Laurel Cove."

"I don't care who they are," said Holly. "She's a dyed-in-the-wool witch!"

"And you're so jealous you've gone bananas!" he said.

"Please take me home, Tyler."

He shook his head. "I'm working on job leads and some good invitations."

"Will you call me a cab?"

"Sure. If you have ten bucks to pay for it."

Trapped, Holly went to the ladies' room. All the women greeted one another effusively as they wielded expensive lipsticks and combed streaked blonde hair. They all ignored Holly, who dawdled there as long as she dared. Heading back to the main hall, she paused in the doorway, feeling as shy as a child at her first day of dancing school.

Carlotta was on the dance floor, crushed to the ruffled chest of a stout, grey-haired gentleman. He whirled and bobbed unsteadily to the beat of "It Was Just One of Those Things," his eyes closed and a happy smile on his florid face. Carlotta had a forced smile on her lips.

When Holly tried speaking to a few of Craig's friends, they nodded vaguely, wouldn't look her in the eye, murmured an excuse, and edged off.

Tyler steered completely clear of her.

The evening became torture. Holly didn't know if she was allowed to sign for a drink, and she didn't dare ask.

A staircase led off the dance floor. Maybe Archibald hid his clue here, she thought, mounting to the ninth step. She sat, surreptitiously patting the gleaming floorboards for cracks, but afraid to examine the area too openly.

Finally, after what seemed like hours, Holly saw Craig at the bar and threaded her way around the crowded dance floor to him. "Can we go home?" she asked.

"Home?" He blinked down at her. "What for? Thought you wanted to dance."

"I have a headache."

"Lil' dance'll cure you." He gulped at a beer and reached for her. "C'mon, Holly."

Rather than make a scene, she complied. To her embarrassment, he clasped her closely and forced a clumsy two-step to the rock rhythm. For once, Holly did not physically respond to him. His hands felt clammy, his awkwardly aimed kisses reeked of whiskey, and he hummed off-key in her ear.

But not the tune played by the band. Instead, Craig hummed the all-too-familiar Christmas carol:

> *The Holly and the Ivy . . .*
> *When they are both full-grown . . .*
> *Of all the trees that are in the wood,*
> *The Holly stands alone.*

Was this a drunken coincidence?

"Fun, eh baby?" He tried to spin her around, crashed into a nearby couple, and staggered. "Wheee! Floor's slippery!" He lurched back to the bar and finished his whiskey-laced beer. "Another!" he roared to the bartender.

It was horrifyingly similar to Holly's memory of the barn dance. Only this time she was twenty instead of six. As people began to stare, she darted over to Craig. "You've had enough!"

"Don't *you* tell me to stop, my good woman!"

While the music continued to blare, Holly was wondering how to get him out quietly when Dr. Phipps strode over. "I'll drive him home," he called over the music.

91

But Craig frowned. "Home?" He focused on Dr. Phipps with difficulty. "Can't go home. No party there."

Dr. Phipps put his arm around Craig's shoulders. "Come on, pal."

Craig shrugged him off. "Leave me 'lone."

"Please, Craig?" Holly was near tears.

He jerked his thumb. "Phipps'll take you home. I'll stay with Audrey."

"But you can't drive." Visions of her mother's car hurtling over Lyon House cliff made Holly feel close to hysteria.

"I'm fine," Craig insisted. "Won't go home."

"Want me to call the Commodore?" Dr. Phipps asked.

Craig took a swing at him, missed, crashed in a heap on the floor, and passed out.

Chapter 14

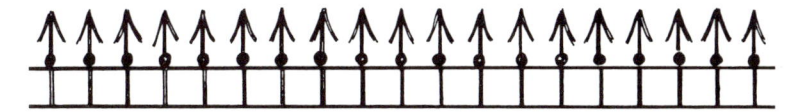

The band stopped, and the ensuing applause sounded farcical—as if it were for Craig.

Quickly, the orchestra swung into a loud jazz piece, as Dr. Phipps knelt and loosened Craig's tie.

"My God!" Tyler spoke in a strained whisper. "What if one of Grandfather's trustees sees this?"

"What happened?" Carlotta asked.

Tyler pantomimed gulping from a glass.

"He's violent!" Holly screamed over a loud fanfare of drums. "He tried to hit Dr. Phipps!"

Heads turned. "Who the hell is *she*?" someone asked.

Carlotta winced. "Hush," she said sharply to Holly.

"But—" Holly started.

"Cool it!" Tyler snapped. "You'll get Craig thrown out of the Club. Want that on your conscience, too?"

With that, he and Carlotta propelled her out to the parking lot and pushed her into the Mercedes. Then Tyler headed back indoors.

Carlotta's voice shook as she started the car. "Men don't want women around at a time like this. I know, because occasionally my Edward had a few too many. Fortunately, Bud Phipps knows what to do. We'll go home."

In her bedroom, Holly dejectedly pulled off the pink gown. She'd assumed that a formal date with Craig would mean a glamorous, possibly perfect evening. How childish she had been! He was obviously in love with Audrey. And Tyler had warned her, but Holly had chosen blindly not to listen. But why did he have to choose tonight to get drunk?

Too upset to sleep, she settled into bed with a book. Her eyes were tired, and a headache threatened. Annoyed, she recalled leaving her reading glasses in the glove compartment of Craig's car.

She turned out her light, her restless brain a kaleidoscope of thoughts. If tonight indicated what her father and grandparents had endured with her mother, small wonder the old Vermonters wanted no contact with the Lyon family! Yet their feelings, she realized, were not confused by infatuation.

She loved Craig when he was sober, loathed him when he was drunk. Almost as if he were two different people.

Had her father felt the same way about her mother? Had he ever told her mother how he *really* felt about her drinking? Or was alcohol a silent monster that lurked between them—omnipresent but unconfronted? Holly wished with all her heart that her father were still alive, so she could talk to him about this.

Some time later, hearing the faint hum of a car, she hopped out of bed and saw a station wagon disappear behind the house. She heard the crunch of footsteps on gravel as the car headed back down the hill.

Had Dr. Phipps brought Craig home?

She stared out over the harbor. Lights winked from yachts anchored in the cove, and an occasional power boat puttered slowly among them. Holly felt remote and painfully lonely. It was ironic to think that at this very moment perhaps someone was admiring Lyon House from an anchored boat—wondering enviously who lived in such a grand mansion.

Soon she saw more headlights: Tyler's Jag. When a light went on in the library, Holly leaned over the sill and saw him step alone onto the terrace. Clasping his hands behind him, he stared out at the view. The Heir Apparent, Holly thought with disgust.

Now a third car zoomed up the hill. Headlights jerked from side to side. The car veered dangerously close to the cliff, swerved just in time, and Craig's Porsche skidded around the house. She heard gravel spurt, brakes screech, a car door slam, then unsteady footsteps.

Tyler hurried in. The library lights went out.

Once again the old house was silent. Holly didn't want to see Craig again in his drunken state, but she was still too keyed up for sleep, and she would develop a worse headache if she read without her glasses.

She put on a robe, grabbed a flashlight, and slipped downstairs. Hinges squealed as she pushed the heavy door open. Were eyes watching her? Was that soft breathing in the phone alcove?

Tiptoeing across the graveled courtyard in her sneakers, she heard rustles in a rhododendron. She paused, trying to believe it was just some small creature in the underbrush.

Faint moonlight revealed something near the garage. Had someone dropped a jacket or sweater?.

She snapped on her flashlight, then stared incredulously. Patches of blood glowed red against the grey pebbles. The remains of the Siamese cat, Gning, lay directly behind a rear wheel of Craig's Porsche, its entrails completely flattened by the weight of the automobile.

Holly gagged with revulsion. Her legs buckled as she turned, stumbled, and ran back to the house.

She had loved that cat. So had Craig. But he was so drunk tonight the he hadn't even noticed the animal!

She raced back up to her room, spurred by a terror greater than anything she had felt this summer. How often had her father confronted the ravages of her mother's drinking, culminating in that final, terrible night?

With blinding clarity, Holly knew that she must get away from Lyon House. At once, before she risked repeating the family tragedy with Craig Lyon. Sobbing raggedly, she stuffed her belongings helter-skelter into her suitcases.

Glancing around the rosebud room she had grown to love, she whispered, "Goodbye forever. I have to be a Blake again if I want to survive."

She lugged her bags downstairs. As she headed for the telephone, she sensed another presence in the vast hall. But she was too angry to be afraid, even when she saw a patch of white behind the giant elliptical archway.

A voice said softly, "Miss go away?" It was Saito.

"Mr. Lyon ran over Gning tonight," she said, no longer bothering with pidgin English. "He killed that beautiful cat, right by the garage."

Saito shuddered and disappeared into the dining room.

Holly phoned for a taxi. Then, aware that Murray was a night owl, she called him at home. "Sorry to bother you so late," she said. "But I'm quitting the *Gazette*."

"Oh *no*! Why, Holly?"

"Because of Craig," she said. "I'm catching the next train home to Vermont."

She jumped into the cab while the driver was loading her luggage. "The railroad station, please," she said.

"Your butler wants you," said the driver.

"It's not important. Let's go."

Holly didn't look back. Both she and her father had found love here at Lyon House, and both had suffered heartbreak as well. But while her father's final trip down this driveway had resulted in death, Holly was determined to remain alive.

The quaint Laurel Cove train station was deserted. A posted timetable announced that a train was due in twenty minutes, so Holly sat down on a bench to wait.

A familiar battered station wagon drew up and Peter emerged, carrying a thermos. "Want some coffee?" he asked.

"What on earth are you doing here?" Holly gratefully took a cup of the strong, steaming brew.

"Murray told us you were leaving." Peter opened a bag of glazed doughnuts, and said, "I really hate to see you go."

"I have to." She bit into a doughnut, swallowed with difficulty, and put it down on her lap, shaking her head.

Peter settled on the bench beside her. "Craig get home okay?"

She stiffened. "Why do you ask?"

"I just saw a couple of Club stewards at the Hamburg Nook. They said he really tied one on."

"Did he ever!" Holly spoke savagely. So the news was out.

"Did he hurt anybody?" Peter asked.

She nodded. "He ran over our Siamese cat."

"Gning?" Peter gulped at his coffee, and Holly burst into tears. "Not the guy you thought you were in love with?" Peter's tone was mild.

"*No!*" she sobbed. "I can't *stand* him any more!"

"Shattered dreams department. So you run away," said Peter.

Holly glared at him. "Don't play little mind games with me!" She blew her nose. She could hear a faint train whistle in the distance. Tomorrow night she would be home in her bunk bed with her Pooh bear. She'd be treated like a child, which was exactly what she wanted.

"Your Grandparents know you're coming home?" Peter asked.

Holly shook her head.

"What if they've gone on vacation?"

She hadn't thought of that. The drugstore was too busy summers to allow time for real holidays, but occasionally the Blakes managed a weekend with relatives in Canada.

She spotted a pay phone, found coins, and dialed. "Grandpa? It's Holly!"

"Well . . . ," The familiar, but sleepy, voice made her feel even more homesick. "It's one a.m.! Where *are* yuh? Is something wrong?"

"I'm at Laurel Cove," she said. "I'm coming home."

"You drunk?"

"No. But you were right, Grandpa. I shouldn't have stayed here."

"They hurt yuh?" His voice was gruff.

"Not physically." *Yet*, she added to herself, but that part could wait. "I found out about Mother. There are others like her, Grandpa. I don't belong at Lyon House. I want to be home with you and Grandma." The ensuing silence made her uneasy. "Can you still use me in the drugstore?" she added hesitantly.

"Gave yer job to another girl. She's got yer room, too."

Holly felt a flash of resentment. "But Grandpa—"

"When you make a decision, you stick by it," he said flatly. "B'sides, don't you want yer shot at that estate?"

She knew it would be useless to argue. She'd let Grandpa down; he had every right to make new arrangements.

She sank back down on the bench. "He gave away my room," she told Peter, wondering where she could spend the rest of the summer.

"That's rough."

"How would *you* know?" she asked scornfully. "With your happy, no-hangups family?"

Peter threw back his head and roared with laughter.

"What's the big joke?" Holly snapped.

97

"I've been where you are now," he said quietly. "You see, Dad's an alcoholic."

"Royal?" Holly gasped.

Peter nodded. "Brandy for breakfast. Brawls in bars. Jails. Hospitals. And he's hurt me—badly. My twelfth birthday, we'd planned a ski trip to New Hampshire. Mom and I waited all day with our gear piled in the front hall. Dad finally showed at midnight, dead drunk. He'd totaled the car, and what's more, didn't remember doing it. Didn't even remember it was my birthday!"

Holly thought of her own sixth birthday, that her mother had never lived to celebrate with her. "What did you do?"

"Emptied my piggy bank. Took off for New York, with thirteen bucks. Knocked around the East Village for a few days, till the cops finally phoned Mom. That's when she separated from Dad."

Peter's grey eyes were gentle behind his tortoise-shell glasses. Holly had been too preoccupied all summer with Craig to realize that Peter was quite good-looking, too.

"Seven years ago," he continued, "Dad joined AA. Hasn't had a drink since. The family's together again, as you know."

Envy snaked through Holly. "You can't raise the dead," she said bitterly.

"No, but you *can* help the living."

"Isn't Craig too young to be a real alcoholic?" she asked.

Peter snorted. "Alcoholics aren't just old bums scrounging cheap wine. Kids as young as twelve join AA when they find they can't handle booze. And alcoholism is progressive. Next time Craig'll do something worse. Have a car accident, maybe kill a person instead of a cat."

"Like my mother," Holly murmured.

Peter nodded. "Back then, nobody looked for alcoholism in teenagers. Doctors didn't even know that a big capacity can be a warning signal."

"I don't want it to happen again," she said intensely. "I don't want to be killed like my pa."

The station bell clanged. Roadway gates lowered. Holly stood, forgetting she had no destination.

"Holly . . ." Peter raised his voice over the noise of the bell. "Would you help your mother if she were still alive?"

"How do I know?" she cried impatiently as the train's headlight appeared far down the track. "She doesn't sound like much of a mother."

"Too *sick* to be a good mother," Peter said. "Once she started drinking, she couldn't stop."

Involuntarily, Holly began to comprehend some of her mother's crazy behavior at that square dance. And her reckless abandon the night she was killed.

"Your Dad's mistake that night was trying to make her stop drinking," said Peter.

Now Holly understood. She hadn't driven home with Craig this evening, thanks to Carlotta. If Julia had driven alone that night, Holly would have at least *one* parent alive today . . .

Peter spoke into her ear as the train whistled loudly. "Craig needs help, Holly."

She stiffened. "That's Audrey Woodward's problem. Craig's in love with her." She zipped open the safety compartment of her bag, to see if the ten-dollar bill she kept for emergencies was still there.

"Audrey would never agree that he had a drinking problem," Peter persisted. "But *you* could—"

"Peter!" Holly cut in sharply. "Don't you get the message? I *loathe* Craig Lyon!"

As the train drew to a halt, he asked bluntly, "Do you hate him, or his disease?"

Peter sounded like that phrase in Archibald's letter:

> I hope that you will not blame me for your mother's problems, Holly, but will come to realize that she did, indeed, have a disease.

She pictured the reaction of Archibald's ghost if she boarded this train with nineteen dollars and eighty-eight cents. Hardly more than Peter had taken when he ran away to New York as a kid! And Holly was in no mood to knock around the East Village.

"If Archibald were here now, what would he say?" Holly asked.

"He'd tell you to use your head and history won't repeat itself," he said. "Mr. Lyon was a neat guy. Really interested in young people. He'd probably ask you to try Lyon House again,

99

for just one day. Anyone can do anything for one day.''

The Archibald Lyon despised by Craig, Carlotta, and Tyler would have wanted Holly at Lyon House for vindictive purposes. But the Archibald Lyon that Peter knew seemed kind and gentle, like the author of Holly's letter. *That* Archibald Lyon wouldn't have wanted Holly to come to any harm, and might even have wanted her to inherit everything.

Wouldn't she be a fool to pitch a possible inheritance so impulsively? Especially since she had just noticed that Peter Meade was an attractive young man?

"If you change your mind," Peter added. "I'll bring you back to the same train tomorrow night."

Chapter 15

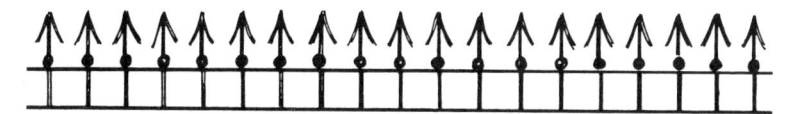

Holly spent the rest of that night in the Meades' unpretentious guest room. The next morning, after Mrs. Meade cooked a hearty breakfast, Peter drove Holly back to Lyon House. Tyler was entertaining someone in the library, but no one else seemed to be home, so she changed into shorts to search again for Archibald's "clue in the ninth step."

In front of the mansion, a flagstone path roughly resembled steps. She was counting nine flagstones down from the terrace when Mimi called to her from the driveway. "Okay if I use the bicycle?"

"Sure," Holly called back. Normally she rode it to church on Sunday mornings, but today she'd overslept.

Mimi took off at a fast clip on the old bike. Too fast, Holly thought, for directly ahead, the driveway dipped sharply for its steep descent to the cliffs.

"Careful!" Holly called.

The bike rolled faster.

Mimi gripped the handlebars, her body hunched forward, hair streaming in the wind, feet spinning wildly on the pedals.

Alarmed, Holly shouted, "Hand brakes!" and started dashing across the lawn.

Now the bike was hurtling full speed downhill. In a few seconds, Mimi would reach the cliffs.

"Turn it!" Holly screamed. "Turn, Mimi!"

Mimi wrenched the handlebars. The bike careened wildly between two laurel bushes atop the precipice.

"Jump!" Holly shrieked.

Mimi flung herself to the ground. The bike wavered crazily on the clifftop, miraculously righted itself, and rolled away down the drive.

"You okay?" Holly gasped, arriving at her cousin's side.

Mimi lay still. Her face was pale, but her eyes were open.

"Any broken bones?" Holly asked.

Mimi gingerly moved her arms and legs, then shook her head. ". . . feel sick. . . ." she said faintly.

"I'll call a doctor," said Holly.

Mimi shook her head again. "Don't."

"Hey!" Tyler called from the house. "Anybody hurt?"

"Mimi!" Holly shouted.

"Be right down. Dr. Phipps is here."

Mimi struggled to sit up. "Stop him!" she said urgently.

"For heaven's sake, *why?*" Holly asked. "You've just had an accident! He's a doctor!"

"He'll ruin everything." Mimi sank back down as Bud Phipps, wearing a white tennis outfit, sprinted down the hill. Tyler was close behind.

Dr. Phipps knelt and quickly examined Mimi. "No broken bones," he announced.

When he bent lower Mimi murmured something in his ear and glanced at Tyler with wide, frightened eyes.

"How far along are you?" Dr. Phipps asked bluntly.

"Two-and-a-half months," Mimi whispered.

"I'll give you some mild medication." As Dr. Phipps rummaged in his black bag, Holly sat down beside Mimi, stunned.

"So my baby sister got herself pregnant." Tyler towered over Mimi, his long arms folded. "Thank God, Mother's out. Will you give me the name of a gynecologist, Bud?"

"Sure thing." Dr. Phipps handed Mimi a small white pill. "I know a good man in Locust Valley. He's awfully discreet."

Mimi clenched her fists. "No operation, Tyler."

Dr. Phipps glanced at his watch. "Let's take her up to the house," he said.

Holly ran ahead to prepare Mimi's four-poster bed. She pulled off the heavy taffeta spread, fluffed the pillows, and took the silver water carafe to the adjoining bathroom. She'd closed the door to freshen up when the others arrived in the bedroom.

Dr. Phipps' loud voice carried through the door. "I can arrange—"

Mimi murmured something.

"Follow orders," said Dr. Phipps. "Stay in bed . . . excuse me, tennis game . . . send your maid up. . . ."

Holly was wondering uncomfortably if she should emerge, when she heard a door shut, and Tyler said in a low angry voice, "Have a *baby*? . . . baby yourself!"

Mimi sounded angry, too. "I'm nearly twenty."

"Shhh!" hissed Tyler. ". . . the father?" he asked.

"Not a 'preppie'," said Mimi. ". . . not in any clubs."

Holly started involuntarily. Peter Meade had attended public school. Not in the club set. She thought of his surreptitious meeting with Mimi at the beach party. Unabashedly, she eavesdropped through the bathroom door.

"Local gold digger," said Tyler.

"Nice . . . ordinary . . ." said Mimi. "And *I* love *him*!"

Peter was a nice, ordinary boy. *Very* nice, in fact, Holly thought dismally.

"Dime a dozen!" Tyler's tone was urgent. "Your education . . . the right people . . ."

"I don't like Mummy's friends." Mimi's tone was bitter. "Or yours. Can't you accept that?"

"Flipped out!" Tyler sounded furious. ". . . tell Mother tonight."

"You'd do *anything* to win!" Now Mimi sounded like Carlotta. "I'm not the baby you think I am! I want this estate, too. If you say anything, I'll tell Mummy about the missing silver!"

Tyler muttered something in a menacing voice.

". . . inventory Grandfather's Gorham . . ." said Mimi.

"*Shut up!*" Tyler said.

"I'll shut up if *you* will!"

Holly could feel years of rivalry crackle between them. But these stakes were adult ones. If Mimi felt she must hide a pregnancy from her own mother, and Tyler was stealing family silver, then Cousin Archibald's estate must be large indeed. So why shouldn't she fight hard for it, too?

"Where's Holly?" Tyler's question prompted Holly to ease open the opposite door and tiptoe into Aunt Prissy's bedroom, thankful that the old lady was still in the hospital. Out in the hall, she crept quickly down the long corridor to her room.

Just as she reached for her doorknob, Tyler burst out of Mimi's room. "Where were you when we put my poor sister to bed?"

"Getting something from Aunt Prissy's room!"

Tyler glanced at her empty hands. "Remember that *you* have something to hide from the trustees."

Holly gaped at him.

"I saw you take off in a taxi last night and return with some guy at ten-thirty this morning." Tyler's tone was triumphant. "You violated Grandfather's will."

When she had accepted Peter's invitation, Holly had completely forgotten about spending all nights under the Lyon House roof.

"So we'll have to trust one another, won't we?"

"Excuse me." Holly shut her door in his face.

A few minutes later, she strolled down the beach staircase. Nobody seemed to be around. She'd examined the ninth step from the top earlier this summer. Today she poked with a trowel at the hard dirt underneath.

She repeated this under the ninth step up from the landing, the stair where the nylon line had tripped Aunt Prissy, the ninth step down from the landing, and the ninth step up from the beach.

She'd reached the bottom of the staircase before she noticed Craig sunbathing at the far end of the beach.

"Sweetie!" he called. "Come sit." He patted his giant scarlet towel, emblazoned with the Lyon House crest. White trunks accentuated his great tan.

Her heart led her. Holly perched crosslegged beside him, told him about Mimi's accident, then asked, "How do you feel?"

"Lousy." Outsize dark glasses masked his eyes. "About last night—darling, I'm awfully sorry."

His mouth looked vulnerable. Holly painfully recalled their kisses, and felt unwelcome stirrings of the old attraction.

"Did you hear about Gning?" Craig added.

She nodded.

"Poor little bugger," he said huskily.

Holly's throat closed up. "You were driving like a demon."

"I don't even remember driving home," he said. "Have to watch my boozing for a while."

"Why not quit?" she blurted.

"What for? I'm not an alcoholic."

Holly stared uneasily at him. If he could run over a beloved pet and not remember doing it, could he throw a boulder, attack someone on a cliff, and a stretch nylon line across a stair—without remembering anything the next day? "What more proof do you need?" she asked.

"All I did last night was tie one on," he said. "*That* doesn't make me an alcoholic. Everybody gets zonked once in a while."

"Do they all stage brawls? Pass out on the dance floor?"

"Whoa, baby!" he laughed shortly. "I got a little out of control, but—"

"Maybe next time you'll crash your Porsche over the cliff!" she cut in quickly.

Craig's dark glasses glittered in the sun. "What's with you today? Why lay your mother's drinking problem on me?"

"I'm sorry," she said stiffly.

"It bugs me whenever anyone says I can't handle booze," said Craig. "Dad used to claim that a *real* man could control his drinking. One night, I blew up. Told him my drinking habits were *my* business. He said that if I couldn't drink like a gentleman, I was no longer welcome at Lyon House." Craig's voice was husky with emotion. "Next day I went to Spain. Never saw the Old Man again. Sent back all his letters unopened. . . ." His hand shook as he lit a cigarette. "But the old s.o.b. got the last word with that crazy clause in his will."

"Does your crowd in Europe drink a lot?" Holly asked.

Craig shrugged. "No more than here."

Thinking of her mother's wasted life, Holly asked softly, "Do you have fun?"

He gazed out over the harbor. "Yeah," he grinned. "Fantastic blasts. Whopping hangovers to go with 'em." He chuckled. "Expatriate living, baby. Sangria for breakfast and all that jazz."

Royal used to drink brandy for breakfast. . . .

"Sure, I drink too much sometimes," Craig continued. "My capacity isn't what it was at Harvard."

"What about hurting others?" Holly asked in a small voice.

Craig got up and began pacing the beach. "Poor old Gning . . ."

Holly held her breath. *Now* would he see?

"By the way," he said, "Audrey was in a real sweat about your wrecking her dress."

"I'll apologize to her, Craig. Something hit me, and I literally didn't think."

"I probably should have gone on home after she changed, but she didn't want to miss the dance."

Waves lapped the shore. As Holly watched a trio of gulls patrol the water for fish, Craig started kicking seashells like a small boy.

"I'd hate to blow Dad's estate," he said. "Maybe I should quit—until September, anyway."

"You want help?" She tried to make her tone diffident.

"What sort of help?"

"There's an AA meeting in Laurel Cove."

He stopped short. "If I walk into that meeting, I might as well climb the village flagpole and announce that I'm an alcoholic!"

"It's Alcoholics *Anonymous*," she pointed out.

He shook his head vehemently. "People always talk in a small town. I could never drink around here again, even after Dad's estate is settled. Anyway, I'm not an alcoholic."

"Why do you keep *saying* that?" asked Holly.

Craig kicked a stone so hard it flew out of sight down the beach. "Because I can stop drinking when I really want to, damnit!"

Holly scooped a palmful of sand and watched it run through her fingers. His denial must be based on feeling that Lyon money and social position would protect him from the results of his drinking. She got up. "Be sure you explain that to the family when you bury Gning," she said.

"Wait!" He grasped her shoulders. "Last night was unusual. Have you ever seen me like that before?"

She shook her head reluctantly.

"Take my word it won't happen again? I'm a grown man. Give me one more chance?"

His brown eyes were pleading. His hands slid around her shoulders, but this time Holly felt cold. She thought of last night, then of a Plymouth coupe hurtling over the cliff, her parents trapped inside. . . .

Were all alcoholics this stubborn? Did they always cause the people they loved this much pain and confusion?

She jerked away from him, suddenly wanting to pay him back for last night. "Aren't you giving the pitch to the wrong girl?"

"Holly, please. . . ."

But she couldn't stop. "Try the chick with the trust fund!"

With that, Holly took off. She had decided to stay, but she told herself firmly that it was *not* because of Craig Lyon.

Chapter 16

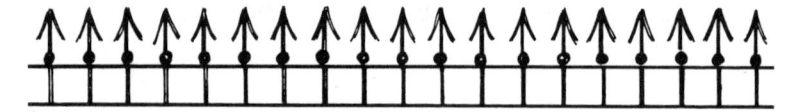

Aunt Prissy came home from the hospital that evening, limping with an ebony walking stick. "Didn't like the sound of Mimi's accident," she announced. "What happened?"

Carlotta kissed the old lady. "Mimi found some decrepit old bicycle with no brakes." She shuddered and took a deep swallow of her martini.

"That Schwinn's a grand old machine," Aunt Prissy protested, as Holly helped her into a chair. "I've ridden it clear to the village."

"Excuse me." Saito appeared in the door. "Bicycle here. Su Chen bring from woods."

"Throw the damn thing away!" cried Carlotta.

Craig strode into the room. "It wasn't an accident," he announced grimly. "The brake line was cut."

"My God!" Carlotta gasped.

"Who would want to harm Mimi?" croaked Aunt Prissy. Her eyes darted to Tyler, who stood by the fireplace, a gibson halfway to his lips.

As Holly thought of Tyler's quarrel with Mimi that afternoon, Carlotta whispered brokenly, "Mimi could have been killed."

"Was *intended* to be killed, you mean," said Craig savagely. "Our driveway goes straight down to the cliffs."

"*I* always start braking up by the house," said Aunt Prissy.

A chill flicked down Holly's spine; she herself loved to swoop fast down that drive, braking at the last minute for the sharp turn. Anyone at Lyon House could have observed her. But who?

"You use that bike, don't you, Holly?" asked Craig.

She nodded, noticing that he was drinking a Coke. "Sundays, for church. The brakes were fine last week."

Tyler swung around. "So you doctored them before you split

with all your luggage, knowing you wouldn't be the victim!''

Aunt Prissy thumped her stick on the Aubusson carpet. "What's this?"

"Didn't anyone else see Holly leave here late last night?" Tyler asked.

"Holly, dear!" Carlotta exclaimed. "I hope you have an explanation."

The long room pulsed with tension.

But Holly challenged Tyler's hostile gaze, thinking of the missing silver. "I just *stole* away for a while," she said, adding, "I changed *my* mind, however."

A faint flush stained Tyler's cheeks.

"Only Holly and I ever rode that bicycle," snapped Aunt Prissy. "And I've been in the hospital all week."

Swift comprehension sparked Craig's eyes, but before he could speak, Saito announced, "Phone call, Miss Holly."

She ran out. This latest attack didn't frighten Holly—it made her furious.

"A royal bird told me you're still in town," Murray greeted her on the phone. "Want to be a full-time reporter at a hundred and fifty a week?"

Fifty dollars more than her secretarial salary! "How can I be a country reporter without a car?" she said.

Murray chuckled. "There's an old Volkswagen you can use. But," he added gruffly, "you pay for your own gas."

"It's a deal," she said happily. "Thanks heaps, Murray."

"You deserve it," he said.

The family had gone in to dinner. When Holly announced her news, there were no congratulations, even from Craig, who said instead, "So Holly's to be the target."

"For what?" she asked.

"We know you're flattered, dear," said Carlotta hastily, "But you're young and naive. Easy to delude."

"It's a promotion!" Holly protested. "Same salary as Craig."

Craig flushed. "I don't trust Murray. What do we know about him, except that he somehow wangled control of the *Gazette* for the summer?"

"Flattering you now, Holly, dear," said Carlotta, "could assure Murray his job in September."

"If Holly wins the estate," added Tyler.

Holly knew that Archibald's estate included the newspaper. Nevertheless, their remarks were like a dash of icy water. "Murray specifically said that I deserve the promotion," she said defensively.

"He'd say anything to keep you on staff," said Tyler. "I was too smart for that ploy."

"And just what worthy endeavors have *you* been up to?" Aunt Prissy glowered at her great-nephew.

"*La crème*, Auntie." Tyler deliberately wiped his lips on his napkin before continuing. "Phil Woodward asked me to crew for him."

"Tyler, darling!" Carlotta beamed at her son.

"Congratulations," Craig said heartily. "*Aristocrat*'s a damn fine boat. Stands a good chance to win the Commodore's Cup."

"Phil's father was my beau the summer of 1915," said Aunt Prissy. "I was the envy of the whole North Shore."

"I remember Phil, Senior," Carlotta said. "A real catch. *All* the Woodwards are." She winked at Craig.

"Even though we know the Woodwards so well, I was watched carefully before Phil signed me on," said Tyler proudly.

Craig nodded. "Woodwards don't take just *anyone* for crew."

No, thought Holly, you have to be elected to the Yacht Club, just for starters. And born into the Social Register decades before that.

Craig, Carlotta, and Aunt Prissy raised their glasses in a toast to Tyler before saluting one another. The red wine in their glasses glowed like blood; spookily, even a sombre ancestor in a portrait behind Tyler held a goblet aloft.

Although Holly shared the Lyon blood, she felt like an outsider during this family ritual.

Tyler, his hard blue eyes softened by candlelight, might be a real reprobate, but his was the triumph of the evening. Yet triumph for what? For stealing family silver, so he could pander full time to a North Shore society leader? Was *this* what Archibald had in mind? And would they remain loyal to Tyler, no matter how ruthless he might be? Even if he was a potential murderer?

"Incidentally," said Tyler casually, "I'm pretty sure Phil's a trustee of Grandfather's estate."

"How come?" asked Craig sharply.

Tyler shrugged. "Little hints he's dropped at the Club. . . ."

"Thank heavens you've spent so much time there!" said Carlotta fervently. "It's really paying off. And now you'll sail with him every weekend until September." Her eyes shone. "I'll call Audrey for golf tomorrow."

As Suito created a Caesar salad, Holly wondered if Craig would also hasten to make dates with Audrey. And would Tyler drop any hints to Mr. Woodward about Mimi's condition? Or Holly's night away from Lyon House?

If so, Holly could retaliate with the missing silver.

The next week passed quickly for Holly. Murray was so pleased with her articles that he granted her a byline. Thrilled, she mailed several clips to Vermont, hoping her grandparents would be proud of her.

She began evening reporting one night when Murray phoned Craig at home.

"I give Murray an honest eight-hour day," Craig complained to Holly. "What does he want—blood?"

"I think the party sounds like fun," Holly said.

"Not me. Political bashes can be pretty liquid, and I'm embarrassed when I turn down booze." Craig gestured to the Coke at his elbow. "Haven't had a real drink since the Club dance, and I'd rather not be tempted."

Now that she drove her own car to work, Holly rarely saw Craig alone. He spent hours in his childhood playroom tinkering with electric trains, and she thought he looked depressed. "You okay?" she asked hesitantly.

He shrugged. "Sure. Bud Phipps gave me a mild sedative to take three times a day." He smiled tensely. "Not that I couldn't do it on my own, but he said the pills would make me more comfortable."

"Do they keep you from wanting to drink?" Holly asked curiously.

Craig frowned. "I told you I'm not an alcoholic, Holly! I'm just playing it safe until September."

Holly did such a good job on the political assignment that Murray gave her more evening work. By the end of July she was spending scant time at Lyon House except to eat and sleep. Murray continued to praise her work, and as her self-esteem rose, she found that the Lyon family intimidated her less. She even decided that Aunt Prissy's and Mimi's injuries had stopped her adversary.

But she was wrong.

Peter invited her to hear a jazz-rock group. For once, it wasn't a *Gazette* assignment. When Holly came downstairs that evening, he frowned at her shoulder bag. "Better leave that here," he said. "You could be ripped off."

Holly ran upstairs and shoved the bag in her closet.

It was one of those evenings that should have been great: fantastic music, enthusiastic crowd, Peter an expert dancer. Holly noticed several girls eye him with interest. She was attracted to him, too, and she felt increasingly confident that the feeling was mutual.

Until she heard a disturbing conversation between Peter and a girl Holly didn't know.

"How's Mimi?" the girl asked him.

"Still taking it easy," Peter said. "She's allowed out for work, but not at night."

"Poor kid," said the girl. "What's she going to do about—"

"Shh!" Peter gestured at Holly, who pretended to be absorbed in her beer. "Mimi's cousin," he said.

The girl pulled Peter out of earshot.

Was Peter the "nice ordinary" guy that Mimi had discussed with Tyler? The father of her unborn child? Was Peter dating Holly tonight only because Mimi was still an invalid? Or, as Craig and Carlotta had intimated, was Holly being exploited by Murray for future *Gazette* aims, with Peter's cooperation?

On the way home, Peter drove into the Laurel Cove beach parking lot. When he switched off the car lights, Holly was in the mood to be kissed. Her heart pounded expectantly.

"Have a good time?" he asked huskily.

"Oh, yes!" She turned eagerly to face him.

He removed his glasses, tipped her chin up, and leaned forward.

His lips were inches from hers when Holly suddenly remembered about Mimi. "Do you think people ought to be faithful, no matter what?" she blurted.

"What do you mean?" Peter sounded surprised.

If he was innocent, she mustn't divulge Mimi's secret. "Say someone's emotionally involved." Her voice was strained because his fingers still held her chin. "Maybe for the wrong reasons, but say there's—oh—a family responsibility or something. Should they fool around with other people?"

Peter pulled away from her. "Family responsibility," he repeated uneasily.

He stared at her for several moments as a symphony of crickets filled the air. Then he put his arms around her in a clumsy bear hug. "I wouldn't want you to cheat on me," he murmured. "And by the same token, I'll play fair with you."

She snuggled briefly against him, then whispered, "That's the way I feel, Peter."

"If things ever change, let's talk," he said in an unhappy voice, kissed the tip of her nose, and started the car.

Audrey Woodward's silver Mercedes was parked in the Lyon House courtyard. Holly grimly leaped out of Peter's car with a fumbled thank-you-for-the-evening.

A second evening turned to dust. A dreary track record, perhaps, but only four weeks to go before Archibald's will would be revealed. Then she could return to her old life.

She saw a crack of light under Mimi's bedroom door and hurried by. No point in talking about Peter to his secret girl friend. She reached her bedroom, glad at least that she had a great job to look forward to in the morning. Bless Murray for giving her the chance to learn newspaper reporting, even if he had devious reasons for doing so.

As she started to place her shoes in the closet, she noticed that her shoulder bag was sitting on top of her evening sandals. Certain she hadn't left the purse there, Holly zipped open the safety compartment.

It contained her emergency money and her car keys. But Cousin Archibald's letter was missing!

Chapter 17

Beginning the next morning, Holly noted signs of the same investigation that she'd conducted all summer for the "ninth step:" fresh tacks on the front hall staircase carpeting and on the linoleum-covered back steps; disturbed dust on the attic stairs; footprints in the black earth under the beach staircase.

Sunday afternoon, while she was out, Archibald Lyon's letter was returned to her purse.

Late Tuesday night, when she heard the French doors below her window creak open, Holly jumped out of bed wearing jeans and a black shirt. She'd suspected that the formal garden would be searched that evening, since low clouds blanketed the skies. Sure enough, she could just make out a figure kneeling on the brick steps.

She crept downstairs on sneakered feet, carrying a flashlight, and tiptoed across the gravel courtyard. Near the corner of the mansion, she heard a twig snap. Were two people out there? One to dig, the other a sentinel?

She ducked behind a stone statue, then crawled close to the low wall that bordered the formal garden.

The night was menacingly quiet. Even the crickets were still.

She heard the furtive grate of metal against brick. She inched toward the noise. Leaping up, she aimed her flashlight and snapped the switch.

The glare revealed a crouched figure, enveloped in a black, hooded slicker!

Shielding its face with one arm, the figure half-rose and swung the other arm in a fast arc.

Holly dodged as something whistled past her ear. A trowel clanged against a statue behind her. She hurled herself flat on the ground, her heart hammering against her ribs.

Stealthy footsteps. Would the enemy bound over the wall nearby?

But the footsteps, accompanied by the swish of rubber, grew faint—then ceased.

Cautiously, Holly rose to peek over the wall.

The formal garden was empty. But a sound made the small hairs rise on the back of her neck. From a far clump of spruce came the low, warbling whistle she hadn't heard for several weeks:

> *The Holly and the Ivy . . .*
> *When they are both full-grown . . .*
> *Of all the trees that are in the wood,*
> *The Holly stands alone . . .*

Holly fled to her bedroom, slammed the door and slid the bolt. She had laid herself wide open for this one.

All summer her enemy had behaved like a sneak, staging bizarre attacks that backfired and got other people hurt. Holly was not about to be done in by a coward, but she would not try confronting the enemy directly again. She would keep a low profile, and continue to search for that ninth step clue herself.

Since the clue was in Cousin Archibald's letter, and Holly's link with him had been her mother, she would try next to trace the clue through Julia Lyon Blake. But aside from a few old books and the ivory-backed dresser set, Julia's room seemed to contain nothing personal. Then Holly recalled Bud Phipps' inviting her back to The Manor.

The next day, Dr. Phipps greeted her warmly, then asked how Mimi was feeling.

"She's back at work," Holly told him. "But I'm here about my mother, Julia Lyon Blake. You told me at the Yacht Club that I could see her records."

Dr. Phipps nodded, spoke into his intercom, then smiled reminiscently. "I met Julia Lyon when I was a Yale undergrad. She was a debutante. Marvelous girl. Beautiful dancer. Superb dresser. Life of every party."

Another description of the perfect party girl, Holly thought. "Was she an alcoholic back then?" she asked.

Dr. Phipps stared at her. "Julia could hold her drinks. She never got higher than anybody else."

"What about the night she died?" Holly asked.

Dr. Phipps hesitated. "As a matter of fact, I was at that party. Hadn't seen Julia since she married that dreary teacher from Verm—excuse me, your father. She'd just been released from here. Said she wanted to celebrate, so the champagne flowed like water."

Through his office window, Holly watched patients playing golf, tennis and croquet, and sunbathing by the Olympic-sized pool. White-jacketed stewards circulated with iced tea and sandwiches on silver trays. "Celebrating" seemed a peculiar reaction to leaving such a luxurious place, unless Julia was desperate for the one thing the hospital didn't provide: alcohol.

The receptionist, Miss Francis, came in with a file folder.

Dr. Phipps perused it swiftly. "Insomnia . . . migraine headaches . . . paranoia . . . cramps in the peroneus longus . . . gastroenteritis . . ." He frowned. "Julia didn't feel comfortable in Vermont. Said people didn't like her, that she was a failure as a wife and mother."

"What treatment did she get?" Holly asked.

"Miltown, three times a day," Dr. Phipps said. "That's a mild tranquilizer, very popular at the time. Her doctor prescribed the same medication when she signed out."

"Did she join AA?" Holly asked.

"There's no diagnosis of alcoholism," said Dr. Phipps testily. "Thompson wasn't an alcoholic rehab place then. Besides, she was only twenty-six."

"Kids as young as twelve have joined AA," Holly quoted Peter.

Dr. Phipps snorted. "Just an occasional freak case, usually from the wrong side of the tracks."

"What do you think about Craig?" she asked.

He beamed. "A vanishing breed—your true, upper-class gentleman. Means a lot to a guy who worked his way through Yale to be Craig's friend." Dr. Phipps looked speculatively at Holly. "Craig told me about your accusing him of being an alcoholic."

"What's your opinion?" Holly asked.

117

Dr. Phipps evaded her eyes. "His nerves are shot over losing his old man. He says he drinks to relax. I'm inclined to agree."

Holly's eyes widened. "You saw him that night at the Yacht Club! He even took a swing at you!"

Dr. Phipps shook his head. "You've led a sheltered life in Vermont. Ivy League guys always get a buzz on at events like wedding dinners and school reunions. That dance was a big reunion for Craig."

"Later that night he ran over our cat," said Holly in a choked voice.

"Damn shame. But cats can be replaced."

She could hardly believe her ears. The doctors she knew in Vermont were traditional: kind to people and animals. Was Dr. Phipps using his friendships at The Manor to social-climb?

"If my mother wasn't an alcoholic, then what was wrong with her?"

Dr. Phipps shrugged. "I gave you her symptoms. Call her highly neurotic. Unfortunately, she didn't respond to psychotherapy."

Holly thought of Archibald's letter: "a disease . . . nothing you need be afraid of inheriting, if you guard closely against it."

How could she be on guard, if she didn't know what "it" was? "Will I inherit it?" she asked Dr. Phipps.

He picked up a large paperweight fashioned from a golf

trophy. "Just as Julia couldn't handle her new life in Vermont, you may be finding Laurel Cove uncomfortable. Even threatening."

The word "threatening" hung in the air between them. As he shifted the paperweight from one tanned hand to the other, Holly noticed his long, capable fingers. Despite the doctor's white coat, impressive title of Medical Director, and courteous demeanor, there was something devious about him. But what would Dr. Bud Phipps gain by getting rid of Holly Blake?

"Are there any references to stairs in my mother's records?" Holly asked suddenly.

"No."

"How about the number nine?"

He shook his head and quickly closed Julia Lyon's folder. "Why do you ask?"

"Just something my Blake grandparents mentioned years ago," Holly improvised. "Thanks for seeing me."

"Pleasure, my dear, but leave the diagnosing of patients to me." He opened his office door. "Craig'll be A-okay. He wants to stay sober until September, so I put him on a really effective new sedative. He hasn't been drunk since that night, has he?"

Holly shook her head. "He sits in his room alone every night and reads."

Did a fleeting expression of triumph cross Dr. Phipps' face as he ushered Holly out?

Walking past the dining hall, Holly spotted a Siamese cat curled on a window seat. With its right ear pricked forward, its chin nestled on crossed paws, it looked like Gning napping at Lyon House. Nostalgically, she approached the cat, which opened one blue eye, yowled, then rolled on its back and waved its paws.

Holly tickled the animal on its throat. The cat batted her wrist with its right paw. Holly tickled its left ear, and the cat began to purr.

"Gning!" cried Holly, hugging the animal. "Oh, Gning! You're not dead after all!"

The cat's rusty purr rose to a crescendo and he lapped her ear with his coarse tongue. Overwhelmed, she wept into his short, soft fur.

"Sam?" The receptionist, Miss Francis, called from the doorway. "Oh, Sam-mee! It's kitty's lunch time. Baby want some tuna?"

The cat stiffened.

"I see you—you bad cat!" Miss Francis waggled her manicured nails coyly, then approached, arms outstretched.

Gning arched his back and flexed his claws. "He's my cat," Holly told the receptionist.

"Don't be ridiculous. Sam's mine. Come to Mama, Sam."

Gning hissed and spit. Holly backed away, still holding the animal close. "Gning lives at Lyon House. He just did his favorite trick for me."

"All Siamese cats look alike." Miss Francis advanced purposefully.

As Holly thought of the night of Gning's supposed death—that gory mess on the Lyon House driveway—fear crept up her spine. Why would Miss Francis insist that *she* owned this cat?

Miss Francis reached again for Gning, who streaked out of the room.

Holly drove rapidly back to work, deeply shaken.

Who had staged Gning's fake killing last month, designed to implicate Craig? Holly had seen a station wagon at Lyon House that night. But only one person at The Manor had Lyon House connections: Bud Phipps. He drove a silver sports Mercedes, and seemed to be on friendly terms with all the Lyons. However, he wanted to marry Audrey Woodward—a good motive to harass Craig into leaving Laurel Cove.

But if it *was* Dr. Phipps, why all the attacks on Holly? And why steal Archibald Lyon's letter, unless the Lyon estate was somehow tied in with the Woodward family.

How did Miss Francis fit in? Was she nothing but a loyal employee of Dr. Phipps?

Holly longed to confide in someone, but all the Lyons except Aunt Prissy were on her suspect list. Peter was not only involved with Mimi, but also loyal to Murray; Murray might be trying to gain permanent control of the *Gazette*.

Late that afternoon, at the Hamburg Nook for a Coke, Holly asked Royal for the definition of an alcoholic. She still couldn't get used to the idea that this cheerful, serene man was a recovered alcoholic.

Royal seemed neither surprised nor embarrassed. "Someone whose life is unmanageable—out of control—in *any* area due to alcohol," he said promptly.

"How can a doctor tell if his patient is one?" Holly asked, just as a group of noisy people entered the restaurant.

Royal leaned across the counter. "Supper rush startin', so I can't stop to chat, darnit. Most docs miss the symptoms. A drunk'll lie to doctors and double-talk his way out of every crisis. You're a college girl. Why not go to the library and read up on it?"

The small village library had a surprisingly good stock of literature on alcoholism. After dinner, Holly curled up in the Lyon House library and began to read.

She learned that Craig's amnesia, the night he drove home from the dance, was called a "blackout" and considered a definite symptom of alcoholism. His "Sangria for breakfast" in Spain was another. Some case histories of young people reminded Holly of Craig, as well as of what she'd learned about her mother.

Evidently, The Manor had misdiagnosed Julia Lyon Blake!

She was studying a chemical analysis of alcohol when Craig sauntered in, carrying a can of beer. He took a deep swallow, then made a disgusted face. "I could use a drink of booze for a change."

"Beer's booze," said Holly.

He shook his head. "Not the real thing, like gin or whiskey."

"Yes, it is," she said, then read from her book: "A twelve-ounce can of beer, a table glass of wine, and a bar shot of whiskey all contain the exact same amount of ethanol."

"What's that claptrap?" Craig plucked the volume out of her hands. "Therefore," he read aloud, "even one can of beer can trigger the alcoholic's compulsion to get drunk." He snorted. "You're really bugged about alcoholism, aren't you? Well, you'd better stay off *my* back!" He tossed the book back to her. "I haven't had a real drink since July twelfth. Exactly twenty-four days. However, I *have* had an occasional beer. . . ." He took a deliberate swallow from the can. "Do you see me charging for the gin bottle?"

121

Holly shook her head, reluctant to start another argument. Besides, he had a point: Holly hadn't seen him drunk since the Yacht Club dance.

Later that night, Holly's concern about Craig faded when she learned something about her mother's drinking that directly affected Holly herself. One of the books from the Laurel Cove library was about the fetal alcohol syndrome, also called FAS.

Holly had heard of these birth defects in babies of alcoholic mothers. Tonight she learned that a baby could suffer subtle damage if the mother drank even socially during pregnancy—damage traditionally not associated with alcohol (such as hyperactivity) or unsuspected (such as slightly impaired IQ).

She thought of her mother's elopement with her father. Craig had said that Julia was three months pregnant at the time: Holly was born six months later. She remembered the Lyons, as well as Dr. Phipps, describing Julia during that period as a real party girl—a heavy drinker. Obviously, then, Julia was drinking heavily when she was pregnant with Holly!

How *could* she?

What harm had Julia's alcohol consumption done to unborn Holly?

She started to reread the long list of FAS symptoms, stopping with a small shock at "underweight":

> FAS babies are not only born small, but remain small as children. They have skinny arms and legs. Their parents complain that they can't fatten them up, no matter how hard they try.

Holly glanced down at her own skinny limbs. She knew she had weighed less than six pounds at birth. She was still short for her age. For years, Grandma had nagged her to eat, tempting her with eggnogs, homemade ice cream, and nourishing sandwiches between meals. Holly willingly ate everything offered, but she remained what Grandma called "skin and bones."

Was this a subtle effect of her mother's drinking during pregnancy?

How about that small drop in IQ mentioned? Holly's grades at Vermont Teacher's College were excellent, but she had been turned down by an Ivy League college. Her Lyon cousins attended top colleges. Was this, too, her mother's fault?

Chapter 18

Craig was on the office phone all the following morning, verifying evidence on kickbacks taken by a local politician. At lunchtime, as he opened a can of beer, Holly said, "You shouldn't mix sedatives and alcohol, Craig."

"Holly, please. . . ."

"There's a potentiation effect," she continued quickly. "What that means is that beer and one sedative taken together can have the impact of six to eight."

"Will you please get off my back?" he said irritably. "You're making me feel like a Bowery bum over one lousy beer!"

He ignored her for the rest of the day, left the office early, and was out all that evening.

The next morning at breakfast, she was told he was sleeping off a hangover.

"I can't understand it." Carlotta looked troubled. "He only had a couple of spritzers at the Woodwards last night, but he got high as a kite."

The sedatives, Holly thought.

"He got into the gin later," Tyler reminded his mother.

Carlotta nodded. "I hope Phil Woodward didn't notice."

"The party was pretty raucous by then." Tyler glanced nastily at Holly. "Audrey couldn't keep her mitts off Craig. Made Bud mad as a hornet."

At a quarter to nine, after no answer to her knock, Holly opened Craig's bedroom door. He was fast asleep. She shook him, but he groaned and burrowed deeper into the sheets snoring heavily. Disgusted, but concerned, she stuffed his jumbled notes into a folder, drove to work, and told Murray he was sick.

"I'll bet. Friend of mine was at the Woodwards last night. Did Craig give you the exposé?"

She shook her head. "But I brought his notes. I could write the article."

"Nope. Presses roll in half an hour."

"He's discussed it with me," Holly said. "I could still whip out a short—"

"No," Murray interrupted her. "For once, I want Craig to shoulder the full consequences of a drunk."

At noon, Craig lurched into the office, face awkwardly shaven, wearing one black loafer and one brown one.

"Where've you been?" Murray barked.

"Up late last night. Sorry. Family business." Craig's eyes were bloodshot and his hands shook. He spotted a folder on his desk. "Holly, you're a doll! Did you—did you—" he shot a glance at Murray "—finish checking those details?"

Holly shook her head uneasily.

"I killed the story," Murray said. "You're fired, Craig."

"What?" Craig's voice cracked. "Over this? Dad would have had someone write up my notes!"

"I doubt that," said Murray.

Craig's eyes narrowed. "All summer you've been dying to can me. Picking on me like an old woman."

"With reason," said Murray.

"I've been working damn hard!" Craig protested.

"But you got drunk," said Murray evenly. "*Again.* Blew a major story. Unless you agree to stop drinking, and that includes beer, I won't take you back."

Craig's face turned pale. "Shove it, West. Next month, the Lyons'll have control here. *You'll* have to deal with *me*!"

"Fair enough," Murray said, as Craig stumbled away down the stairs.

That night, Craig's world at Lyon House collapsed.

At dinner, Tyler announced gravely, "We've been posted at the Yacht Club."

"What does 'posted' mean?" Holly asked.

"It means, my little country cousin, that our bills are way overdue," said Tyler. "Until we settle up, we can't use the Club."

"There must be some mistake," said Carlotta. "Will you take care of it tomorrow, Craig?"

Deliberating over a choice of fresh rolls in a woven silver basket, Craig didn't answer her.

"You've been handling the Club account for the whole family, Craig," Tyler said.

"I paid you twelve dollars, Craig, on July the eighth," said Aunt Prissy, "when you brought my chits for two chef's salads to the hospital. Paid you by check!" she added, thumping her fork on the table.

"I gave you my share for June and July," said Carlotta.

"Me, too," said Tyler, as Holly thought with contempt of the missing Lyon silver.

"I haven't set foot in that dump all summer," Mimi said.

"Well, Craig?" Aunt Prissy spoke in her best schoolmistress voice. "Is this just an oversight?"

All eyes turned to the head of the table. Craig looked less disheveled than he had that morning, but his hand trembled as he broke a roll to butter it. "They'll have to wait," he said finally. "September's only twenty-four days away."

"They won't wait," said Tyler. "The family owes two thousand two hundred and forty-three dollars."

Holly gulped. Mimi whistled softly.

"I can't sail again until the account's settled," continued Tyler, obviously furious. "So you'd better ante up *pronto*, Craig!"

Craig shrugged. "No way until September."

"But Tyler *has* to sail!" Carlotta exclaimed. "*Aristocrat*'s winning! Everybody's talking about Phil's crew!"

"Could we ask Mr. Dodd to put a lien on Craig's salary?" Tyler suggested.

"No salary to attach," Craig said. "Murray gave me the axe."

"Where's the money we gave you?" Aunt Prissy demanded.

"For God's sake! That Club's not the corner laundry!" Craig cried. "Lyons have been members since 1903! Why can't they wait?"

"He spent it," the old lady said flatly.

All the Lyons stared at Craig, appalled.

"Craig," Carlotta whispered, "you're a full-fledged, unconditional loser. Even worse than Archibald predicted."

Although the family had bickered all summer, Holly had never

125

before seen them turn in a pack on one of their own. It was horrifying, and she began to understand why Mimi had kept her pregnancy secret.

"Dad—why did you do this to me?" Craig whispered, burying his head in his arms.

At first, Holly felt no sympathy. Then she thought of Peter's remark: "Do you hate him? Or his *disease*?" Perhaps because she'd been the target of Lyon animosity herself, she began to feel sorry for Craig. She no longer wanted to cover his mistakes. But she knew he must face his drinking problem.

Under cover of further loud family debate, she asked Craig, "What on earth did you do with all that money?"

He raised his head, his dark eyes full of pain. "You'll never understand my world, Holly."

"No matter what world you're in, Craig," she said softly, "it's the first drink that gets you drunk."

For the rest of the week, Lyon House was fraught with tension. The Yacht Club refused to permit Tyler to sail. Craig didn't come home for dinner or the evening all week.

On Friday, Carlotta arrived at the *Gazette* with Tyler, Phil, and Audrey Woodward. Filing papers in a nearby cabinet, Holly could hear their conversation through Murray's slightly open office door.

"I'm going to buy the *Gazette*," Mr. Woodward told Murray.

"As you know, Mr. West," said Carlotta, "when we asked you for a loan on Tuesday, we needed money for some short-term financial matters. Mr. Woodward was a life-long friend of Mr. Lyon's, and we all agree that Mr. Lyon would have approved this idea."

"I don't agree," said Murray.

"Please don't be difficult." Carlotta's tone was gently diplomatic. "Mr. Woodward's offer is most generous."

"We'd get the paper back in two weeks anyway," said Tyler arrogantly. "So what's the difference to you?"

"Arch left me in full control until September first," said Murray. "The paper's not for sale."

"Then we'll force you out," growled Mr. Woodward. "You refused to hire Tyler in June. You've treated Craig like a lackey. I think you're sabotaging the entire Lyon family to gain permanent control of this newspaper yourself. That's the *real* reason I'm offering to buy, West.''

"Take me to court," said Murray coldly. "In the meantime, *I* control the *Gazette*, and there's work to be done. Good morning.''

Quickly, Holly slid a file drawer shut, catching her skirt. Before she could move, Tyler asked nastily, "Eavesdropping again, dear cuz? Whose side are you on this week?"

That night, Holly covered a formal Chamber of Commerce dinner. On the way home, in the pouring rain, the Volkswagon stalled and wouldn't start again. Holly glanced with exasperation at the instrument panel.

Her eyes widened. The gas gauge registered empty. She'd filled it that afternoon, and driven only twenty miles since. If the tank had sprung a leak, she'd have smelled gas at the parking lot. Unless someone had siphoned it off. Someone who knew she was driving alone to the village tonight.

Rain drummed on the car roof. She was in deep woods, miles from both the village and Lyon House, but if she waited until the storm ended, she'd be an easy target.

Slipping off her evening sandals, she picked her way to the blacktop road. Jagged lightning split the dark sky. She was terrified of thunderstorms, and everyone at Lyon House knew it.

Thunder mingled with moaning winds. Holly dodged flying boughs and began to limp from pebble cuts on her bare feet. She breathed in short, ragged gasps. She was wet from the skin out.

After a couple of endless miles, the storm suddenly abated. The wind died down, and the rain changed into a soft, swirling mist. Sinking down on a rock, Holly wiped her bruised feet on her drenched evening skirt, and wrung the water out of her hair. The road and surrounding forests were now hushed.

Then she heard a rustle in the underbrush, followed by the cautious *pad . . . pad . . . pad . . .* of footsteps.

She stiffened. Was it a wild animal? Or a person? She strained to see, but the fog was too dense to distinguish anything farther than a few feet.

Pad . . . pad . . . pad . . .

Huddled motionless, Holly began to tremble. In this eerie,

impenetrable mist, so like the night she'd been attacked on the Lyon House cliff, something *human* was following her.

A twig snapped behind her. She jumped, stifling a yelp of fright.

Another rustle. Footsteps again. Closer now.

Pad . . . pad . . . pad . . .

Now she heard the faint hum of an automobile. Was it friend? Or foe? She glanced wildly around. Her only escape would be into the woods, hampered by a long, wet skirt. A pursuer with a flashlight could easily follow.

And if the automobile driver failed to find her, whoever was stalking the woods would succeed!

A chill flew up her spine. Nobody would hear her cries for help on this desolate road.

Who was behind this nightmare? Who had remained hidden for two weeks, and then decided to strike again tonight?

Chapter 19

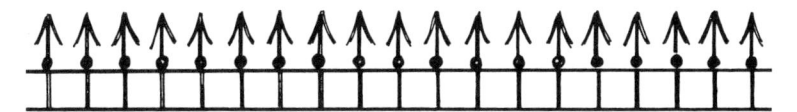

Holly crouched behind a bush until an unfamiliar beat-up Chevrolet emerged through the mist. Too relieved to consider the dangers, she leaped to the road, flagged down the car, and wrenched open the door. "Can you give me a lift three miles up Harbor Road?" she blurted.

"How about all the way to Lyon House?" asked Craig. As Holly turned to flee, he grasped her wrist. "Wait! I saw your Volks, Holly. What's wrong?"

"Come off it. You planned it perfectly, Craig."

He gaped at her. "Planned what?"

"Siphoning my gas tank!" she said.

He stared at her wet hair, soaked and torn evening skirt, bare feet. "What are you talking about?"

The rain began again. Shivering uncontrollably, Holly said, "I'm too tired to run any more. Tell me what you want, Craig."

"You." Craig pulled her firmly into the car and helped her into a cashmere pullover.

Warm at last, Holly burst into tears.

Craig gathered her into his arms. "I didn't siphon your tank, sweetie."

Holly thought of his alcoholic blackouts. "Maybe you don't remember doing it," she sobbed.

"I'm clean—at least for today," he said quietly, holding her close. "May I explain?"

She nodded against his chest, praying that he could somehow clear himself.

"I joined AA six days ago. Haven't had a drink or a pill since," he announced. "I went to an AA meeting in Cold Spring

Harbor tonight, and then to Howard Johnson's for ice cream with Royal and another guy."

Holly lifted her head incredulously.

"It's the most important thing I've ever done," he said. "But don't mention it to the family yet. They'll try to talk me out of it."

His face was inches from hers. Holly's blood quickened.

"I owe you an apology, darling," he continued. "You made me see the truth. After those sedatives, trying to drink socially at the Woodwards was like playing Russian Roulette. I lost complete control—couldn't stop."

"You forgot Murray's warning?" Holly asked.

He nodded. "And everything else, except drinking. Holly—active alcoholism is literally like being insane. If Carlotta hadn't been there, I would have driven home in a blackout—maybe run over a person this time, instead of Gning. Or crashed over the Lyon House cliff, the way your mother did."

They sat quietly for a moment, each wrapped in thought.

"Do you think Mommy wanted to get sober when she went to The Manor?" Holly asked in a small voice.

"I'll bet she did." He hugged her close. "And I'll bet she loved you very much, Holly. You're a pretty special person. But remember, they gave her tranquilizers when she left. Then she went to a party to 'celebrate.' A couple of drinks and wham! She couldn't think of your sixth birthday or how much she would hurt you, or anything else—except getting more booze."

"That's why she drove back to Lyon House for the whiskey, and quarreled with Pa about going back to the party?" Holly asked sadly.

He nodded. "She wasn't just the selfish party girl we all thought she was. She had my *disease*: alcoholism. Once I pick up a drink, there's no way I can predict whether or not I'll get drunk that night. Sedatives or tranquilizers put an atom bomb on the odds."

Holly thought of her research on the fetal alcohol syndrome. "Could Mommy have been an alcoholic at nineteen?" she asked hesitantly.

"Sure," he said. "Looking back, I was in trouble at Harvard.

Spent half my time drinking at the A.D. Club instead of studying."

"But can't an alcoholic stop drinking for *anything*? Even if she's damaging an unborn *baby*?" Holly burst out.

The expression in Craig's eyes shifted from pained to protective. He gathered her close in his arms. "Holly, darling, doctors didn't know that fetal alcohol syndrome existed when Julia was pregnant with you. They didn't even know that alcohol could harm an unborn baby. Besides, what makes you think you *were* affected?"

She held out one arm. "Too skinny," she said.

He kissed the crook of her elbow. "Slim," he corrected her, as their lips met.

Holly knew at once that the old magic was back—for both of them.

Then, abruptly, Craig drew away. "I almost forgot," he said shakily. "My sponsor says no emotional involvement yet. I have to concentrate on the AA program."

She thought of his unpredictability, his moods, his lifelong friendship with Audrey. Was this a ploy to hold her off until he found out who would win the estate? Or was she being unfair to a man who genuinely wanted to get well? Could she ever really trust him?

"I'll be around until September," she said stiffly.

"I'm going to become a decent man, Holly. You'll see."

The next morning at breakfast, Craig handed Tyler a paid-in-full receipt from the Yacht Club. "Thank God!" said Tyler. "I can race this afternoon!"

"How did you manage?" Carlotta asked Craig.

"Sold my Porsche." A muscle jumped in Craig's cheek. "I'd like to apologize to everyone. Someone else can take over the account. I won't be using the Club for a long, long time."

The final two weeks of August, Murray kept Holly so busy that she barely had a moment to herself. She didn't mind. Sure now that journalism instead of teaching was what she wanted after graduation in June, she was eager for the experience.

Murray had rehired Craig, and Holly was astounded at the change in the man. He was prompt for work, friendly to everyone on staff, and conscientious about details. He ate lunch daily at the Hamburg Nook, and told Holly that he attended AA meetings every evening. But although he was courteous to her, he showed no romantic interest.

Friday before Labor Day weekend, her final day at work, Murray gave her a bonus and a glowing letter of recommendation. "You're always welcome here," he said.

"Thanks," she said, moved. "I hope you'll stay, Murray."

"We'll see." He smiled thinly.

Labor Day weekend at Lyon House felt like D-Day. The dispostion of Archibald Lyon's estate would be announced that Sunday evening, and Holly planned to leave Monday morning. Grandpa Blake had written compliments about her articles, and he'd as much as welcomed her back home by saying that her room now would be vacant.

All the Lyons were privately obsessed with the outcome of the will. Tyler strolled about the house like Lord of the Manor, studying charts of Long Island Sound in preparation for Saturday's Commodore's Cup Race. Mimi fingered furniture and artifacts, as if gauging their worth. Aunt Prissy was pink with pride over the second prize she'd won for her roses in the North Shore Garden Club Flower Show, and hinted that more extensive planting should be done next summer. Craig became involved again with Carlotta in running the house. Bickering was at a minimum. Everyone behaved like children being good for Santa Claus before Christmas.

However, Holly was keenly aware of the hostility and tension pulsing under their surface politeness.

She wished she could have one final—really super— night out in Laurel Cove. She even considered phoning Peter, but when he had invited her out these past two weeks, she had turned him down, and he would be leaving next week for college, anyway. Mimi's waistline was thickening, and Holly wouldn't go out with Peter unless he or Mimi leveled about what had gone on between them, and how it was to be settled.

That Saturday, Aunt Prissy was giving a tea for her Garden Club. Holly was in the kitchen trimming bread crusts for finger sandwiches. Aunt Prissy, in the adjacent butler's pantry, selected silver from the walk-in-safe.

"There are fifty ladies coming, so we'll need the large tea service," Holly heard her say. "Mr. Lyon kept it on the top shelf."

"Not here," said Saito.

Aunt Prissy gave an exclamation of annoyance. "Get off the ladder. I'll have a look." Holly heard the rattle of silver, then Aunt Prissy's voice raised in anger. "The whole tea service is gone! Saito, what do you know about this?"

"No take silver!" said Saito, as Holly thought of him in the Glen Cove drugstore with Su Chen and Mimi's redheaded friend, furtively exchanging money. She tiptoed across the kitchen.

"This safe wasn't broken into," Aunt Prissy snapped. "You or Su Chen must have stolen the silver."

"Su Chen no take!"

"Oh, for pity's sake!" Aunt Prissy's imperious tone reflected a lifetime of dealing with servants. "I'm calling the police," she barked. Holly could hear her cane thumping on the floor, then a strangled gasp. "Put . . . down . . . that . . . knife!"

"No call police."

Holly darted into the butler's pantry. Aunt Prissy was brandishing her ebony cane at Saito, who held a long silver carving knife.

"Call the police!" Aunt Prissy cried dramatically.

"*No take silver!*" said Saito quickly.

Aunt Prissy hobbled to the phone and began dialing.

The swinging door to the dining room burst open. "Drop that phone, Aunt Prissy," Mimi said.

The phone receiver clattered to the floor. Mimi and Saito exchanged looks. Holly stiffened. So they were accomplices! Thinking back rapidly, Holly could see how, between them, they had staged the boulder throwing, the attack on the cliff, the fishing line on the beach house steps, the trowel hurled from the garden, the siphoned gas tank. How could Holly and a lame old lady defend themselves?

Cautiously, Holly sidled toward the kitchen door.

"Let the silver-polishing go, Saito. Aunt Prissy thinks you're threatening her with that knife," said Mimi.

Saito laid it on a counter.

Aunt Prissy clutched her spare bosom. "I'm too old for histrionics, Mimi. Why won't you call the police?"

"Because they'll deport Saito if they find him here," said Mimi crisply. "His new visa didn't come through."

"Good riddance!" It was Tyler, sportive in a yacht-racing outfit. "The police can escort him to a plane or boat for the Orient."

"Then I'll go, too," Mimi said.

"With that *thief*?" Tyler barked.

"Saito's no thief, Tyler, and *you* know it!" Mimi flashed back.

"Saito filched our family silver!" said Tyler. "He's a typical, devious, light-fingered foreigner! Should never have been allowed into this country."

Saito glided smoothly over to Tyler, his hand raised in a karate chop.

"Wait!" Mimi leaped between them. "Tyler Lyon, I demand an apology!" Her voice quivered with rage. "You have just insulted your brother-in-law. Saito and I were married last April!"

There was a stunned silence.

"Not . . . Peter Meade?" Holly asked.

Mimi shook her head. "Heavens, no! Peter's just a pal. His cousin is my gynecologist in Glen Cove."

"But Saito's a—a *butler*!" Aunt Prissy gasped. "And he's already married to Su Chen!"

"And you're expecting his . . ." Tyler's voice trailed off incredulously as he glanced at Mimi's waistline.

"Damn *right*! I'm *proud* of it! I—"

"Please let me speak for myself, Mimi." Saito's usual pidgin English was replaced by the impeccable Oxford accent Holly had heard in the Glen Cove drugstore. "Su Chen is my sister. I'm a graduate student at Sarah Lawrence College. Mimi and I fell in love last year."

"I suppose her being an heiress had nothing to do with it," said Tyler hoarsely.

"Indeed not." Saito spoke with dignity. "I'm in love with your *sister*. With her excellent mind, with her tender heart, with her compassion for all people, regardless of their background."

Mimi put her hand into his. "We have our own apartment in Bronxville."

Tyler glared at Saito. "If you're such a hotshot academic, why are you masquerading as a butler?"

"Su Chen asked me to come last May, after Mr. Lyon's first heart attack," said Saito. "Then, as you know, she needed help for the summer. Mimi and I need the money." He put a protective arm around Mimi.

"Did you, sister dear, drop in here last May?" Tyler asked. "Maybe find out why Grandfather wouldn't invite mother or me to Lyon House for two years? Make up with Grandfather, but keep it a secret?"

"I wish I had," said Mimi. "Saito says Grandfather was super. But I guess I was too busy with exams."

"About that missing silver," said Saito. "It's in a Manhasset antique shop. The owner told me that you, Tyler, sold it to him last month. And," he added menacingly, "if you're contemplating disputing my word, the owner is one of my countrymen."

"Oh, Tyler," said Aunt Prissy. "I thought you'd learned your lesson when they expelled you from Groton after taking that boy's camera. Saito, please accept my apologies, and my best wishes for happiness with Mimi." She smiled uncertainly at him. "And now, if you don't mind, can we continue with preparations for my tea party? We could use the Limoges. . . ."

"Jolly good idea." Saito grinned at her.

"Tyler," said Aunt Prissy sternly, "please help Holly chop the eggs. We'll deal with your transgression later."

"Won't you be late for the race?" Holly asked Tyler in the kitchen.

He looked annoyed. "We had an accident."

"Anybody hurt?"

"No. We ran aground on a sand bar."

"You were the navigator, weren't you?" Holly persisted. Because *Aristocrat* was a locally well-known yacht, this could be news for the *Gazette*.

"Will you *shut up*?" Tyler grasped her roughly by the arms. "I am *not* going to tell your paper what happened, Miss Snoop," he said in low tones. "And I don't want you asking anyone *else*, either. Phil claimed it was my fault. I didn't know that Grandfather's charts were twenty years old, for God's sake! But if Phil's a trustee of Grandfather's estate, this means I've had it. And with Mimi's stunning news, which Aunt Prissy will never keep to herself, my *sister*'s had it. That leaves Craig, who'll be scuttled for being plastered so often in public; and Aunt Prissy, who's too senile to manage a vegetable patch; and . . . and . . . *you!*"

Holly recoiled as his blue eyes glittered with hate.

"But," he continued, "there are still more than twenty-four hours left before Dodd arrives. You haven't won yet!"

Chapter 20

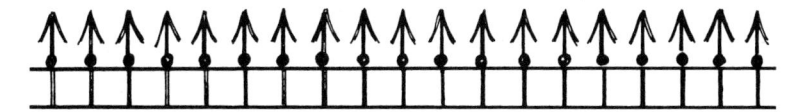

At dinner that night, Aunt Prissy produced a bottle of vintage Piper Heidsick champagne, "for this last, formal, family meal."

As Craig lifted his water tumbler for the ritual family toast, Aunt Prissy asked, "Where's your champagne, Craig?"

"I'm not drinking tonight, Aunt Prissy."

"You look tense," said Carlotta. "A small glass of wine will relax you."

"No thanks, Carlotta."

"Don't be a spoilsport," said Aunt Prissy. "I saved this bottle for a special occasion."

Holly felt a flash of annoyance. Now she could see for herself the social pressures facing a recovering alcoholic. "Craig had an upset stomach this morning," she told Aunt Prissy. "So did I. No champagne for me either, thanks."

After that, any pretense of festivity was dropped.

First, Carlotta read the riot act to Tyler. Chastened, he agreed to ask the Manhasset antique shop owner to hold the silver until the Lyons could buy it back. Then, Tyler was to invite Phil Woodward to dinner at the Yacht Club the following evening and apologize formally for his navigational goof.

"Be sure you're back here on time," Carlotta finished. "Mr. Dodd and the trustees are due at eight o'clock."

Holly thought Tyler deserved stiffer punishment. But if Mr. Woodward was a trustee of Archibald's estate, this must be a last-ditch effort to make amends.

Next, Carlotta turned to Mimi. Her disappointment in her only daughter was so acute that Holly couldn't help feeling sorry for the woman. "History proves that interracial marriages don't work," she said nervously.

137

"Unless he's important, like a U.N. diplomat," said Aunt Prissy.

"But I *love* him!" Mimi protested, as Saito silently withdrew from the dining room.

Carlotta leaned forward. "Even if *you* were happy, Mimi, is it fair to bring an innocent child into such a prejudiced world?"

"I didn't ask to be brought up *your* way," Mimi said. "I agree that Laurel Cove would make mincemeat of an interracial kid. But we're not going to live here."

"I should hope not," said Tyler.

"Mimi dear," said Carlotta, "you're too young to know what you're doing. As your mother, I simply cannot approve—"

"You can't stop the marriage!" Mimi said. "Or the baby! I'll be twenty on Tuesday, remember? I'm an adult."

"Then I'll have Saito deported tomorrow!" Carlotta snapped.

"Mummy!" Mimi sprang to her feet, burst into tears, and ran into the kitchen.

"That was a bit harsh," said Craig.

"Being a Lyon involves serious responsibilities," said Carlotta. "We have to be on guard against gold diggers and social climbers."

"Right, Holly?" Tyler murmured.

"For God's sake, Tyler, please be pleasant for the rest of the meal!" said Craig.

"Why?" said Tyler. "Why masquerade any more, Craig? In exactly twenty-four hours, one of us will win!"

The grandfather clock in the library bonged eight times.

Craig reached for the champagne bottle, filled his glass, and raised it to his lips.

"Don't!" Holly leaped to her feet and snatched clumsily at his glass. Pale yellow liquid spurted across the Belgian lace tablecloth.

"Here we go again," said Tyler. "Carrie Nation doing her thing."

"Craig," said Aunt Prissy, "grab that bottle. Holly's gone crackers."

As Craig reached for it, Holly popped the bottle behind her back. Her eyes locked with his. "Is it worth it?" she blurted desperately. There was such naked misery in his eyes that she added quietly, "Where's Royal?"

"At the Brookville meeting," he said. "But Holly, I wanted to be with you tonight."

She willed herself to say steadily, "Please go to the meeting instead, Craig. I'd rather you did."

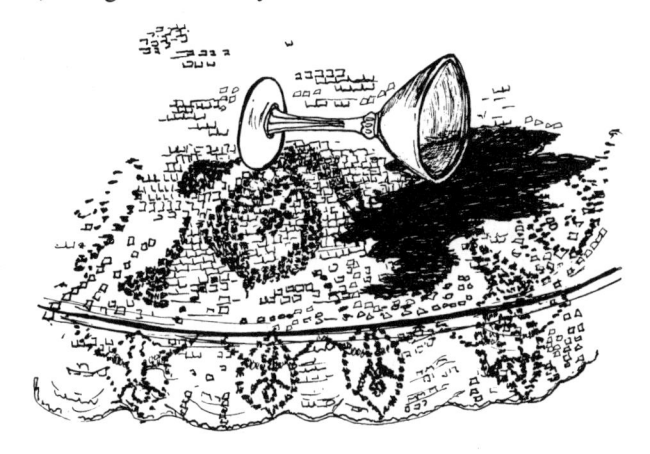

The next morning, Holly phoned Peter. "I owe you an apology. Mimi told us about Saito. I thought it was you."

Peter chuckled. "I just recommended an obstetrician in Glen Cove. Redhead who works at Mimi's farm stand drove her over."

So that explained the surreptitious drugstore meeting, Holly thought.

"Mimi's a good kid," Peter added. "And Saito's a heck of a nice guy. I'm off to college tomorrow, Holly. Good luck tonight. Whatever happens—you've turned into a darned good reporter."

All day, the atmosphere at Lyon House was charged with tension. Holly wished she could let off steam with a long walk, but she didn't dare. Murray had reclaimed her Volkswagen, so she was stuck at the mansion.

After lunch, Tyler departed on his reparations mission. Craig told Holly he had to go out, but would join her later for a swim. She wandered into the formal garden with a book, remembering the trowel attack. Little question now that her enemy was Tyler. Had he been any more successful than she in finding the "clue in the ninth step?" She hoped that Archibald had mentioned what was "rightfully hers" in his final will, in case Tyler had already discovered it.

She thought about tonight. Would the anonymous trustees closet themselves with Mr. Dodd, discuss each Lyon in depth, and then vote on which one deserved the estate? Or would it be settled before they arrived?

She saw Mimi drive off with Saito and Su Chen; then a friend of Aunt Prissy called for her in an ancient chauffeur-driven Packard. Baking in the hot sun, Holly fell asleep.

At six, Carlotta woke her. "I'm fixing a light supper," she said. "It'll be just you and me and Craig. I figured you'd be too nervous to eat much." She laughed shortly. "I know *I* am."

Carlotta could be quite thoughtful when she chose. Tonight she'd fixed Holly's favorite Salade Nicoise, with the chilled vichyssoise and fresh hot corn bread Craig loved.

"I almost forgot," Carlotta said. "This came while I was out, and you were dozing in the garden." She handed Holly a *Gazette* envelope.

Inside was a memo 'From the Desk of Murray West,' typed with a characteristically cryptic message:

> Meet me at the office at 6:30 p.m. I've found a box of old Julia Lyon letters.
>
> Murray

"Take my Mercedes," Carlotta offered. "And hurry back, dear. We'll save your dinner."

The *Gazette* office was empty, although Murray's battered typewriter was uncovered and his ashtray full of cigarette butts. Holly glanced at her watch. The trustees would be at Lyon House shortly; she couldn't wait long.

A few minutes later she heard a faint cry from somewhere in the building. "Holl—ee—ee! Help! Holl—ee—ee!"

Holly stiffened. Was Murray hurt?

She ran to the top of the stairs. "Murray? Is that you?" she shouted.

"Holl—ee—ee!"

She raced down two narrow flights of stairs, yelling "I'm coming!" At the basement landing, she fumbled with a light switch that refused to work, then felt her way slowly to the bottom of the steps. "Where are you?" she called.

A low moan answered her from a far corner.

The narrow windows, tucked horizontally under the ceiling, emitted just enough light for her to make out the bulky printing presses. Threading her way between them, she bruised her shins several times before she reached the corner.

"Where are you?" she repeated, squinting into the darkness.

Her answer was spine-chillingly familiar, this time played on a flute:

> *The Holly and the Ivy . . .*
> *When they are both full-grown . . .*

She spun around, the hair rising softly on the nape of her neck. She'd been tricked! By Murray? Or had Tyler left the fake message at Lyon House?

She'd better get out of this basement—and fast!

Peeking cautiously around a printing press, she tried to plot a course of escape. But her enemy could be hidden anywhere—poised to pounce.

She had no weapon. And who would come if *she* yelled for help?

By now, it must be nearly seven o'clock. In one hour, the trustees would arrive at Lyon House. If Holly wasn't there, she'd be eliminated from the contest. After lasting all summer! But that, of course, was the whole point.

Suddenly angry, she crept forward again. Her foot hit a loose floorboard, which snapped through the quiet like a shot. She froze, her heart pounding in her ears.

The mocking flute began again, accompanied by a weird swishing sound.

> *The Holly and the Ivy . . .*
> *When they are both full-grown . . .*

Abruptly, the basement darkened. Holly saw storm clouds through the narrow windows.

Now the swishing sound was coming toward her.

Her mouth dry with fright, she crawled further behind the printing press. The familiar smells of paper and printer's ink reminded her of happy days, when this shop was brightly lit, the printers at work, the machines clattering.

But now, the whole basement was a cavern of terror.

Panic rolled over her in stifling waves. Huddled on the floor, Holly forced herself to take shallow breaths.

The swishing sound started again, headed away from her.

She rose gingerly and peeped around the press. By the light of a street lamp, she saw a shadow on the white-washed wall. Sharply etched, it was a figure wearing a pointed hood exactly like the rubber slicker of her attacker at Lyon House.

She gasped aloud.

The shadow whirled. She saw its arm rise, and a knife emerge from one long, flowing sleeve. Slowly and deliberately, the knife's shadow slid along the white wall toward her, grotesquely elongating as it approached.

Holly's nerves snapped. She screamed at the top of her lungs, then dove back behind the printing press.

Footsteps sprinted away from her. Peeking out, she saw the figure clamber up the staircase, hampered by the awkward slicker.

Had someone heard her shout?

She ducked back down. But instead of voices, she heard gurgling sounds, followed by two scrapes. The far end of the basement brightened.

A rescuer? Hopping up, she opened her mouth to yell, but the sound died in her throat.

The light wasn't rescue. It was a blazing torch, that arced high, then swooped down to the floor. As Holly watched, horror-stricken, flames began to lick a bale of newsprint. Then, like good kindling, the whole bale caught fire.

The hooded figure slipped out the door. Holly heard the bolt snap shut.

She darted forward. The acrid smell of kerosene hit her nostrils. By the light of the fire, she could see that the entire area around the flaming bale was soaked, blocking her way to the stairs.

Smoke billowed around her, stinging her eyes, nose, and throat. In no time this whole basement would be a blazing inferno!

She knew there was no other door. Coughing, she glanced wildly up at the windows, which were barred. Groping frantically, she found a stack of metal linotype bars.

She hurled one. Glass shattered. "Help!" she screamed. "Fire! Help!"

She heaved another bar, continuing to scream for help. The flames and smoke were spreading fast. She coughed convulsively.

How much longer could she last? People rarely drove to the village on Sunday evening; all the shops were closed, even Royal's Hamburg Nook.

She would die here!

Nobody would know until later, when everyone would decide it had been an accident. Except one person.

Reeling with shock and despair, Holly hoisted herself atop a machine under a shattered window. She gulped fresh air into her aching lungs. She wondered how Craig would react when he learned that she was dead. And Grandpa! Grandpa and Grandma Blake would have lost *two* loved ones at Lyon House! This was the last straw, and tears ran down her soot-streaked face.

She was half-delirious when she heard sirens. She thought it was a dream. And when the firemen burst through the door, she wondered vaguely if they knew she was at the far end of the basement. But she was too weak to call out, so she simply waited—huddled atop the machine—and watched them spray the roaring blaze.

Suddenly a man thrust through the group and staggered toward her through the smoke and flames. Lifting her in his arms, he pressed his cheek against hers. "Thank God you're alive!" said Craig.

Holly was so overwhelmed at being rescued that she barely noticed the strong smell of gin on his breath.

But she did notice what he was wearing: a black rubber slicker with a pointed hood, and long, flowing sleeves.

Chapter 21

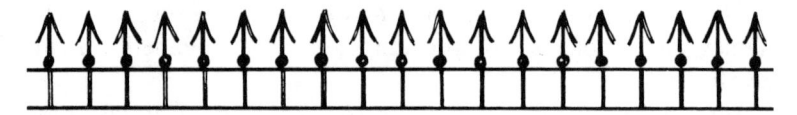

Outside the burning building, Craig said in a slurred voice, "See you later . . . get sherry first," and stumbled toward his car.

"That man . . ." Holly gasped to a policeman, pointing at Craig's beat-up Ford.

"That's Craig Lyon," said the cop. "He just saved your life."

"He set the fire!" Holly cried, as Craig started his motor. "I saw him do it!"

"Miss," said the policeman, "Mr. Lyon himself phoned in to report the fire."

So Craig had lured her here, cornered her with the knife, set the fire, but had second thoughts about leaving her to die. And she had been in love with him!

It was twenty past eight when she arrived back at Lyon House. Mr. Dodd stood, as he had last June, by the library fireplace. Phil Woodward wasn't present, but scattered among the Lyons were Royal Meade, Murray West, Saito, and Su Chen.

"Holly dear!" Carlotta gasped. "What happened to you?"

"Fire at the *Gazette*," said Holly.

Murray leaped to his feet. "I'd better go."

"Fire Department's got it under control," said Holly. "It was in the basement, so your files are safe. But Craig's got to be found. He's gone crazy!"

"Is he drunk?" Carlotta pointed to an empty gin bottle next to Craig's reading chair.

Holly nodded. "He . . . he tried to kill me!"

"*Craig?*" cried Royal. "He couldn't have!"

"Do you think I threatened myself with a knife, threw kerosene around the *Gazette* basement, then set the fire?" Holly demanded.

"I believe you, dear." Carlotta patted the sofa beside her. "Sit here by me."

"Why so sure it was Craig?" Royal asked Holly tersely.

"Because he was wearing a black slicker with a pointed hood when he set the fire," she said. "He was still wearing it when he rescued me. He was wearing it when he attacked me last June on the cliffs, and another night in the formal garden. I'd know that thing anywhere!" She shuddered, and Carlotta put a comforting arm around her.

"Royal and I spent most of the afternoon with him," Murray said. "We're all members of AA. He was uptight, but he vowed he'd leave Lyon House—forfeit the entire inheritance—before he'd take another drink."

"So he changed his mind," said Tyler. "We'd better call the cops."

"Don't!" said Aunt Prissy sharply. "Think of the scandal!"

"Can't we find him ourselves?" Carlotta suggested. "We know his habits. The police don't."

Disgusted to the core of her being, Holly said, "Lots of luck. He's out looking for sherry. How *could* he, after all that gin?"

"Try the Yacht Club," said Carlotta. "And the Harbor Inn."

Murray glanced at Royal. "Come on, pal."

"One moment, please," said Mr. Dodd. "As trustees, you two must be present when I read this will."

"We won't leave the house," said Murray. "We'll phone."

As the two men headed out, Mr. Dodd announced, "This is the last will and testament of Archibald E. Lyon."

Holly's eyes widened in horror at Archibald's portrait. Savagely slashed with a knife, the old man's stern face was hanging in jagged shreds! Had Craig flipped out completely? Would he burn down Lyon House next?

"I, Archibald E. Lyon," read Mr. Dodd, "being of sound mind, do hereby bequeath the ivory statue of the praying hands to my friend, Royal Meade."

"The statue was the most valuable thing Archibald owned!" Aunt Prissy cried. "Why did he leave it to that—that waiter?"

"I'll have the legatee explain." Mr. Dodd sounded irritated, but fetched Royal back into the library.

145

"Archie was an alcoholic," Royal said quickly. "Joined AA two years ago. Never had another drop."

Tyler and Carlotta looked stunned. Now Holly understood why Archibald didn't invite Carlotta and her children to Lyon House for two years: Carlotta and Tyler drank heavily enough to make him uncomfortable.

"What about the statue?" Tyler asked.

"Praying hands can be a symbol of AA. Archie said it was his most precious possession. But not the way you folks might have figured. He meant his sobriety."

"Now I understand the strangers at our Christmas party year before last," said Aunt Prissy.

This also explained the crowd Peter had described at the July Fourth parties, Holly thought, as the telephone jangled. She could hear Murray answer it in the entrance hall.

"Archie's recovery was some miracle," Royal continued. "The guy even *looked* different, you know? After he came in the program, he never stopped smilin'."

Tears sprang to Holly's eyes as she understood at last the discrepancy between the portrait and Peter's photograph. Also, the genuine affection his new friends—Royal, Murray, and Peter—felt for him.

"Enough hearts and flowers," said Tyler impatiently, as Murray beckoned to Royal from the door. "Who wins the estate?"

Mr. Dodd looked flustered. "I need both of you trustees here."

"I have a lead on Craig," Murray snapped. "*We* need your legal advice, Mr. Dodd."

The lawyer placed the will on the mantlepiece and left the room.

Silence descended. All the Lyons gazed at the slim, blue-covered document. The ticking of the grandfather clock dominated the tense atmosphere.

Suddenly, Tyler jumped up, grabbed the will and scanned it. His face turned white. "Holly gets the works," he said.

Carlotta's arm tightened around Holly. "Everything?"

Tyler nodded. "Except the statue, and a bunch of history books for Saito. Grandfather's whole will is only one lousy page!" He slammed it back on the mantle. "Well, Holly, how does it feel to be an heiress?"

Now that the moment she had sometimes imagined was actually here, Holly felt young and scared. What would she do with this tremendous mansion, surrounded by endless land? How could she cope with leaking roofs, old wiring, termites, taxes, pot holes in the driveway?

Must she welcome all Lyons whenever they wanted to visit?

She had occasionally daydreamed about living at Lyon House with Craig. Now that was out. She certainly wouldn't stay here alone, and Grandpa and Grandma Blake would never consider moving from Shelburne.

Why in the name of heaven had Cousin Archibald left Lyon House to her?

"Will you ask Holly for my next year's tuition?" Tyler murmured to his mother. "The bill came last week."

"Later, dear," Carlotta whispered, as Holly realized that she now held the family purse strings. In view of Tyler's attitude toward work, she didn't feel like paying his way at the University of Virginia. But how nasty, or even dangerous, would he be if she refused?

Murray appeared in the doorway with Mr. Dodd. "Telephone for you," he told Carlotta.

As Carlotta hurried out, Tyler edged over to Mr. Dodd. "I saw the will," he said in a low voice. "Does Holly really get everything?"

"That's right."

"But why?" Tyler's voice rose. "She's not a direct descendant!"

"Your grandfather wanted to make amends," said Mr. Dodd stiffly.

"That's the ninth step," said Murray.

"Ninth step?" Holly cried. "What do you mean?"

"We have twelve steps to recovery in the AA program," he said. "The ninth is, 'Made direct amends to such people wherever possible, except when to do so would injure them or others.'"

Holly thought of Archibald's letter:

. . . something very important here is rightfully yours. There's a clue in the ninth step.

He hadn't meant a clue in some staircase! But before she could question Murray further, Aunt Prissy plopped herself on the sofa. "I've been thinking about the old greenhouse," she told Holly. "We could rebuild it quite easily. Then we'd have a nice place to put the geraniums during the winter."

"If you're thinking of improvements," said Tyler, "how about a boat house, Holly? We could build one on the beach. I'll even teach you to sail."

Carlotta stood in the door, looking upset. "Craig's at Rothmann's bar," she said. "He says he'll come home quietly if Holly and I pick him up alone."

"Why me?" Holly objected. "He already tried to kill me once tonight!"

"He's afraid Murray and Royal will have him put away," Carlotta explained. "He wants to come home and sleep it off."

"We'll go with you anyway," said Murray. "We're old hands at this."

"Better not," said Carlotta. "He'd recognize your car and take off. I know how to handle him."

"Why don't we follow in a couple of minutes?" Royal suggested. "In case there's trouble."

Murray detained Holly. "What exactly did Craig say to you?" he asked in a low voice.

"Got to get sherry first," said Holly, quoting Craig, then hurried after Carlotta.

Carlotta drove the Mercedes rapidly down Harbor Road. "Congratulations on winning the estate," she said. "Did Dodd say any more about the will?"

"Only that Archibald wanted to make amends," said Holly. "Murray said that was the Ninth Step of AA."

Carlotta swerved to avoid an oncoming car. "So *that's* the clue!" she breathed.

Busy fastening her seat belt, Holly murmured assent. She felt the hair rise on the back of her neck.

Nobody could know about the clue in the Ninth Step unless that person had stolen Archibald's letter from her. And later heaved a trowel at her from the formal garden. And whistled "The Holly and the Ivy." Someone wearing a black slicker with a pointed hood. . . .

She bit back a yelp of shock. Carlotta had set the fire! Not Craig!

Involuntarily, she gasped aloud, as she quickly saw how Carlotta could have staged every single attack.

"Hmmm?" Carlotta eyed her sidelong, her slim fingers tense on the steering wheel.

"Nothing," Holly said nervously. "Nice night, isn't it?"

It wasn't a nice night. The sky was still heavy with storm clouds, and the wind had risen.

As if she'd read Holly's mind, Carlotta expertly whistled a few notes of "The Holly and the Ivy." Then she guided the car onto a highway.

"This isn't the way to East Norwich," said Holly.

"Craig's not there."

The dark highway flashed by too rapidly for Holly to risk leaping out. But perhaps if they stopped for a red light . . .

"You were after me all summer?" Holly had to know. She had suspected several people recently, and been wrong. Could she be wrong again?

"It was a snap at first," said Carlotta. "You were so terrified when I pushed that boulder down the cliff, I figured you'd be a cinch to scare away from Lyon House. I left that doctor's letter in your room, then swiped Aunt Prissy's slicker and musical instruments for those first little stunts. But then, for some reason, you started getting braver. I had to devise more drastic goodies."

"The *Gazette* fire?" Fear constricted Holly's throat.

"There was so little time left," Carlotta said coolly. "Mimi and Tyler had diced themselves out of the running. I *had* to get rid of you and Craig. Fast."

"But why me from the beginning," Holly asked.

"I'd always assumed Craig would inherit Lyon House," said Carlotta. "Until one night two-and-a-half years ago, when Archibald had too much to drink. Since I always cajoled expensive things out of him when he was drunk, I asked him to leave Tyler a few dozen acres of the estate. Archibald told me that he wasn't the sole owner of Lyon House."

She lit a cigarette with an angry snap of her gold lighter.

"Your grandfather—who was, of course, Archibald's first cousin—inherited half of it," she continued. "When your grandfather died, your mother inherited his half, with money in escrow to pay her share of the taxes. Because Julia was an irresponsible teenager, her father made Archibald her guardian and left instructions not to tell her about the house until she was thirty."

She never knew, Holly thought with a pang.

"I didn't worry," Carlotta continued, "because Archibald never got in touch with you. I figured you were as good as dead. I still assumed that Craig would inherit the house, and share the money with my children."

"Until I turned up last June?" Holly whispered.

Carlotta nodded. "Archibald's will was so bizarre I was *afraid* he'd leave everything to you. What I can't understand," she said furiously, "is why Archibald tricked us all into spending the summer here with no money."

"Maybe he wanted you to get used to coping without it," Holly suggested.

"No way," said Carlotta grimly, turning into the driveway of a small, run-down, frame house. "Welcome to *my* old family homestead. I grew up in this dump, though nobody on the North Shore knows it. The day I married Edward Lyon, I vowed I'd never live like this again."

She pulled a switchblade knife from her purse and clicked it open. "Inside," she said.

Holly walked up the sagging steps. There were no neighboring houses that she could see. If she somehow escaped, where in those open, flat, potato fields could she hide?

Chapter 22

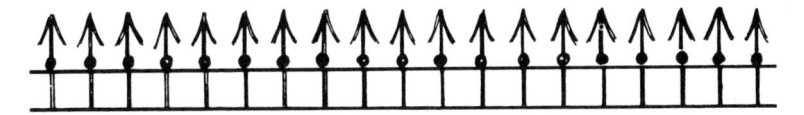

Carlotta pounded on the door. "Sherry?" she called. "I'm here!"

Sherry Francis—Holly recognized her as the receptionist at The Manor—opened the door. "So what happened?" she asked.

"Archibald's trustees turned out to be a couple of AA fanatics." Carlotta shoved Holly into a small, dark living room, its curtains tightly drawn. Craig lay on the flowered carpet, eyes closed, arms and legs bound with ropes. "They fell for my story about Craig being at Rothmann's," she continued. "But let's do some fast planning."

"I got rope from the cellar, like you said," Miss Francis told her. "Who won the estate?"

"Holly," Carlotta snapped, "But don't worry, Sis. You'll still get your cut. My kids will be statutory heirs once these two Lyons are gone." She jerked a length of rope around Holly's arms until the rough hemp bit painfully into her flesh.

"I want plenty," said Miss Francis. "I'm sick and tired of helping you spook this one, and drug that one . . . playing the harmonica in *your* beach house during *your* fancy party . . . and I'm living in this hovel, while *you* lord it up on the North Shore, Carla."

"*Carlotta*," her sister corrected her.

Holly heard a car slow down outside the house. She coughed violently to cover the sound.

With a familiar yowl, a Siamese cat jumped into her lap, rolled on its back, and waved its paws in the air.

"Gning!" Holly cried.

"I thought you got rid of him," said Carlotta.

Miss Francis looked sheepish. "I couldn't. The day Holly recognized him, I brought him home. He's kind of a nice cat."

151

"Good boy, Gning," Holly babbled, rubbing her nose in the cat's soft fur as she heard the click of a car door. "Good, good boy." She raised her voice. "Holly just *loves* Gning!"

"He nearly blew our act," Carlotta said. "We should have used him the night of Craig's fake accident, instead of the dead one from the pound."

"I couldn't kill a healthy cat," Miss Francis protested.

"*I* could," said Carlotta.

Holly heard footsteps rounding the house. She faked another spasm of coughing. Miss Francis pounded her on the back.

"How did Craig get out of Lyon House?" Carlotta asked.

"It wasn't my fault, Sis," Miss Francis whined. "He was still out cold, so I went downstairs to hack up that portrait. Afterwards, I saw him out the window driving away like crazy. Then I heard your Jap butler talking to Mimi, so I figured I'd better get out."

Holly heard a bush rustle outside. This might be her only chance. "Help!" she shouted. "*Help!*"

"Hey!" Swatting Gning off Holly's shoulder, Carlotta grasped her neck with one hand and clapped the other over her mouth. "Is someone there, Sherry?"

Her sister scurried to the window and peeked through the curtains. "Strange station wagon," she whispered.

"Lights!" Carlotta hissed.

The living room went black.

Holly tried to scream again, but Carlotta's grip on her mouth was too powerful. She gagged and began to feel faint.

"Take my knife," Carlotta whispered.

"Oh Carla . . ."

"Take it!"

At that moment, something furry landed lightly on Holly's shoulder. With a blood-curdling shriek, Carlotta released her hold on Holly's neck.

Lights snapped on. Royal and Murray burst into the room. Carlotta reached for her knife, but Murray smoothly flipped her to the floor while Royal lunged for Miss Francis.

Doubled over, Carlotta gasped, "Craig tried to kill my sister. Holly helped. We tied them up in self-defense!"

"Did you get Craig drunk out of self-defense, too?" Royal asked, overpowering Miss Francis with ease.

"You saw the slashed portrait . . . Holly told you about the fire . . ." Carlotta spluttered.

"You admitted *you* set the fire," Holly objected angrily, as Murray snapped handcuffs on Carlotta's wrists.

Using Carlotta's knife, Murray freed Holly. Then he pulled a thin rubber tube from his pocket. "Saito found this in the Lyon House garbage. Stinks of gin. It's an old trick: drugging a glass of lemonade, then pouring the booze down the victim's throat after he passes out. You wanted Craig loaded for the will reading, didn't you, Carlotta?"

"I *told* you to watch where you threw that tube, Carla!" Miss Francis cried, her eyes wide with fright.

"Shut up!" Carlotta snapped. "Don't open your stupid mouth again till I hire a lawyer."

Freed of his bonds, Craig stirred and groaned. Royal fetched a thermos of coffee from the car, held a cup under Craig's nose, and helped him to sit up. As Craig took a swallow, his eyes met Holly's. "You okay?" he asked huskily.

She nodded. "I never thanked you for saving me," she said softly.

"Very touching," sneered Carlotta. "Do you think Craig would have bothered if you weren't an heiress?"

"So you won," Craig said.

Holly nodded again. "How did you guys find us?" she asked quickly.

"I phoned Rothmann's," Murray said. "Craig hadn't been there in weeks."

"Damn right." Craig looked angry.

"So we knew Carlotta was lying," Murray went on. "We discussed Craig's telling Holly: 'got to get sherry first.' As a couple of former drunks, we knew Craig wouldn't want sherry after all that gin."

Craig grimaced. "I meant *her*." He pointed at Sherry Francis. "I needed proof for the trustees that I didn't get drunk of my own accord."

Murray nodded. "Saito figured it out. He'd kept an eye on

Carlotta lately; seen Sherry visit her at Lyon House when everyone else was out. He told me she worked at The Manor. I phoned, and the night girl said Craig had been there at eight, asking for Sherry."

"But how did you know Sherry lived here?" Carlotta asked.

Royal chuckled. "I met her at your weddin'," he said. "I was a waiter. Took her out a couple of times, but she was too ambitious to date a hash-slinger."

"I remembered coming here as a kid," said Craig. "Before you contracted North Shore-itis, Carlotta, and turned your back on your childhood."

Royal stood up. "What say I drive these two ding-a-lings to the police station? Always did say that being a part-time deputy would come in handy."

Murray drove the Mercedes. Holly and Craig climbed in back with Gning.

"Sherry and Carlotta made one vital mistake," Murray chuckled. "Alcoholics have a higher tolerance for drugs than most people. The ladies didn't give you enough, Craig, to knock you out *soon* enough—or for *long* enough."

"I was on the verge of passing out when I heard Carlotta discussing her plans for the *Gazette* fire." Craig put his arm around Holly. "When I came to, I got there as fast as I could. I put on a damp slicker I found in the car—thought it might be some protection against that inferno."

His arm tightened around her. She could feel the old attraction quickening her blood. But she avoided his kiss. Carlotta's voice still nagged at her: *Do you think Craig would have bothered to save you if you weren't an heiress?*

When they reached Lyon House, Holly realized that it was, incredibly, hers now. But even the thought made her feel young, vulnerable, and very, very tired.

They found Mr. Dodd still in the library, with Tyler, Mimi, Saito, and Aunt Prissy.

"Your mother wants you to go to the police station right away," Murray told Tyler. "She and your Aunt Sherry drugged Craig. Your mother set the *Gazette* fire."

"You're kidding!" Tyler looked appalled. "I knew she didn't

like Craig and Holly, but I never dreamed she'd go *that* far. . . . What am I supposed to do?"

Murray shrugged. "Find a lawyer, I suppose."

"Will *you* come?" Tyler asked Mr. Dodd, who shook his head.

Tyler turned to Holly. "They'll want bail. Will you—"

Holly stared incredulously at him.

"No, she will *not!*" Craig exploded. "Don't you realize your mother tried to *kill* Holly tonight?"

Tyler looked at his sister. Mimi shook her head and slipped her hand into Saito's.

"I suppose I could call Phil Woodward," said Tyler.

Aunt Prissy cleared her throat. "He's out for the evening. I spoke to him earlier." Her old eyes were compassionate but firm as she gazed at her great-nephew.

As Tyler Lyon, his shoulders slumped, walked alone out of Lyon House, Aunt Prissy added to the others, "Phil has other matters on his mind tonight. That soap-opera doctor and Audrey are announcing their engagement at the Club this evening during a surprise party for Audrey's grandmother's eightieth birthday."

"They deserve one another," said Craig, winking at Holly. "Will you excuse me while I clean myself up?"

"I'm famished," said Holly. "Anything to eat? I missed dinner."

"Saito and Mimi made a snack," Mr. Dodd said. "I'll wait."

The big butcher-block kitchen table was set with a platter of cold meat and sliced tomatoes, another of bread, and jars of mustard, mayonnaise, and pickles. Everyone including Aunt Prissy and Murray perched on high stools and made thick, sloppy sandwiches.

"Listen," said Holly quickly. "I'm more stunned by Archibald's will than all of you. I don't know how to be an heiress, for heaven's sake!"

Mr. Dodd came into the kitchen. "Miss Blake, I cannot leave without explaining one vital fact." He took a deep breath. "Although Lyon House is yours . . . that's it."

Holly glanced at him, puzzled.

"You mean there's no money?" Aunt Prissy asked.

Mr. Dodd nodded. "Only the *Gazette* profits, which barely cover the taxes here. During the final months of his life, Mr. Lyon lived on his *Gazette* salary."

"Where'd all the money *go*?" Mimi asked incredulously.

"Mr. Lyon spent flagrantly and foolishly all his life," said Mr. Dodd crisply. "By last winter, he was broke."

"So *that's* why no allowances this spring," said Mimi.

Holly felt dizzy with a wild kind of relief. She wasn't rich after all!

"But Lyon House has been legally half yours, Miss Blake, ever since your mother died," Mr. Dodd added.

"Maybe you could sell the house," Murray suggested.

"Only if it were broken up into four-acre lots," said Mr. Dodd. "And Lyon House torn down."

"Oh, *no!*" Aunt Prissy cried.

She and Mimi looked imploringly at Holly, who could tell from their faces how much the demolishing of their family home would pain them.

Royal came in the back door. "The girls are tucked into cots at the jail," he announced. "Tyler's down there trying to throw his weight around, but nobody's paying any attention. Why so gloomy, folks?"

"Mr. Dodd just explained about Archie's estate—or lack of it," said Murray.

Royal nodded. "Arch said once that the happiest year of his life was this last one, when he had to work for a living. If he hadn't took sick, he had an idea for Lyon House which might interest you, Holly."

Su Chen poured Royal a mug of coffee, and he pulled a stool up to the table.

"North Shore needs a place for recovering alcoholics who can't afford The Manor's prices," he said. "Archie used to say that Lyon House would be perfect. Plenty of bedrooms, private beach, lots of land to take long walks...." He looked questioningly at Holly.

"You mean *I* should run something like that?" she squeaked.

"I could." Craig spoke from the dining room door. He had showered and put on a clean white shirt. "I know after tonight that my sobriety is the most important thing in the world to me. I finally read all those letters Mr. Dodd gave me in June; Dad wrote them while I was in Spain, but I'd returned them unopened. I'm on Dad's wave length now, and this is what he'd want me to do. What about it, Holly?"

"I'll be your cook," Su Chen offered.

"Leave the gardening to me," said Aunt Prissy.

"I'll run AA meetings," offered Royal.

"Me, too," said Murray.

"Saito and I can spend weekends and summers here," said Mimi. "I'll plant a super vegetable garden. And Saito can look for a teaching job on Long Island after he gets his master's degree."

Overwhelmed, Holly looked around the table at these people who were dear to her after all. "A pride of Lyons," she thought, suddenly recalling the collective word for lions as she pictured each one contributing a special talent to Lyon House in its new role—a role they all could be truly proud of!

"Naturally, you'll want to work at your own newspaper," Murray said shrewdly.

"Only if you stay as managing editor," Holly said.

"Can't think of any job I'd rather have," he said.

Craig whooped exultantly. Then, as the others buzzed excitedly about their plans for Lyon House, he whispered in Holly's ear, "I have a great idea for your byline. How about Holly Lyon Blake Lyon?" He laughed a little nervously and squeezed her hand.

Happily, Holly smiled at him and nodded agreement, then looked past her family and friends to the window. Outside, the trees spilled shadows—no longer menacing or mysterious—over the long lawn.

She had no doubt in her heart now. Holly Lyon Blake Lyon belonged in *every* way at Lyon House!

157

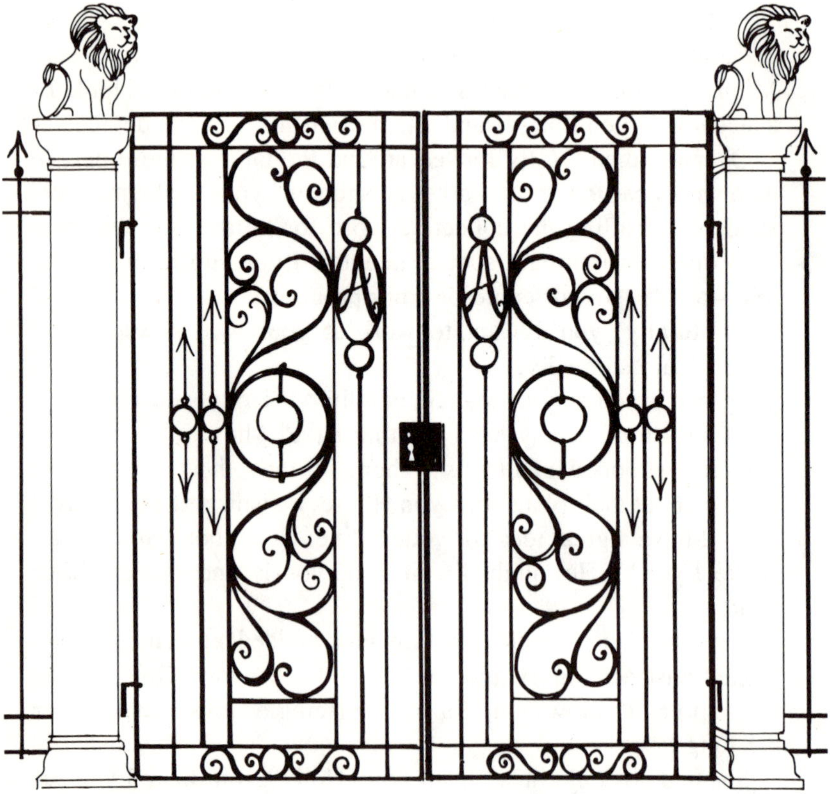

About the Author

This is Lucy Barry Robe's second novel. Her first, *Stagestruck Secretary*, published under her maiden name, Lucy Barry, was based on her experiences as a Broadway secretary. She also is a much-respected medical writer. Her book, *Just So It's Healthy* (CompCare Publications), widely used by schools and colleges as a text, is the first to present in detail, in language anyone can understand, the harmful effects on unborn babies of drinking and using other drugs during pregnancy. She lectures on these dangers to medical and other health professionals and has been interviewed on television and radio talks shows all over the country.

A recovered alcoholic, Mrs. Robe also has given talks for thousands of high school and college students on alcohol and other mood-changing drugs.

She grew up in Boston, where she attended The Winsor School, was a debutante, and graduated from Radcliffe College (part of Harvard University). She has a certificate from the Rutgers Institute of Alcohol Studies.

With her husband and daughter, Mrs. Robe lives on the north shore of Long Island in a village like the one described in *Haunted Inheritance*.

When her daughter, Parrish, was younger, Mrs. Robe was a frequent contributor to *Baby Talk* magazine. Now she writes mainly for professional alcoholism publications and scientific journals.

"Free-lance writing is the best deal I know for answering both the need to contribute as a professional and the strong desire to be a top-notch mother," Mrs. Robe says.

Now that Parrish is in school, and with the help of a supportive husband, Mrs. Robe is able to do some business traveling — usually not more than three or four days at a time — to attend alcoholism conferences and to give lectures and do TV shows.

"But Parrish knows that when I'm home, I'm *there* — to meet her school bus, to play, to entertain her friends. If I have an important deadline that requires extra time, then we'll do our 'homework' together.''

About the Artist

When she drew the illustrations for *Haunted Inheritance*, Mimi Noland, college student, artist and horsewoman, was exactly the same age as the heroine. Like Craig, Murray and Royal in this story, she, too, is recovering from chemical dependency/alcoholism. She described her experiences of becoming addicted to drugs and alcohol, her treatment and recovery in *I Never Saw the Sun Rise* (CompCare Publications). Written at age fifteen under the pen name of Joan Donlan and including her drawings and poems, *I Never Saw the Sun Rise* is unique, the only as-it-happened account of this kind by a recovering teenager. She has heard from many adults and young people in this country and overseas who have gained insights about youth chemical dependency and found hope by reading her book. She now has several years of grateful sobriety.

Her cartoons appear in another CompCare book, *Laugh It Off, some funny, honest ways to help you get serious about losing weight*, by Jane Thomas Noland.

Cover design and title page by Merrily Borg Babcock

CompCare® publications

A Division of the Comprehensive Care Corporation
Post Office Box 27777, Minneapolis, Minnesota 55427

for faster service on charge orders
call us toll free at:

800/328-3330

In Minnesota, call collect 612/559-4800

ORDER FORM

Date _____

Order Number	Customer Number	Customer P.O.	☐ ☐ ☐ ☐ ☐ 1 2 3 4 5	For Office Use Only

UPS 1 ☐	PP 2 ☐	PPD 3 ☐	PPD CHGS 4 ☐	WILL CALL 5 ☐	OUR TRUCK 6 ☐	CARRIER

BILL ORDER TO:

Name _____

Address _____

City/State/Zip _____

Non-profit organization, please show tax exemption number _____

Signature _____ Sales and use tax number _____

SHIP ORDER TO: (If other than above)

Name _____

Address _____

City/State/Zip _____

Telephone _____ Purchase Order (if required) _____

☐ Please ship back-ordered items as soon as possible

☐ Please cancel order for items out of stock

(Catalog number 03145)

☐ Please send _____ copies of *Haunted Inheritance* . . . at $5.95 each.

☐ Please send me the CompCare Catalog of more books and materials for growth-centered living. (No charge.)

PLEASE FILL IN BELOW FOR CHARGE ORDERS
Or enclose check for total amount of order.

Prices subject to change without notice.

Account No (12 or more digits) from your credit card

Check one
☐ VISA   ☐ MASTER CHARGE   Master Charge — also enter 4 digits below your account no

Your Card
Issuing Bank _____

Credit Card
Signature _____

Expiration
Date of Card _____

TOTAL PRICE _____

4% Sales Tax _____
(Minnesota residents only)

Postage & Handling charge _____
Add 75 cents to orders totaling less than $15.00
Add 5% to orders totaling $15.00 or more

GRAND TOTAL _____
(U.S. dollars)

All orders shipped outside continental
U.S.A. will be billed actual shipping costs.

VISA®   **master charge**
THE INTERBANK CARD

CompCare publications ®

A Division of the Comprehensive Care Corporation
Post Office Box 27777, Minneapolis, Minnesota 55427

for faster service on charge orders
call us toll free at:

800/328-3330
In Minnesota, call collect 612/559-4800

ORDER FORM

Date _____

Order Number	Customer Number	Customer P.O.	☐ ☐ ☐ ☐ ☐ 1 2 3 4 5	For Office Use Only

UPS 1 ☐	PP 2 ☐	PPD 3 ☐	PPD CHGS 4 ☐	WILL CALL 5 ☐	OUR TRUCK 6 ☐	CARRIER

BILL ORDER TO:

Name _____

Address _____

City/State/Zip _____

Non-profit organization, please show tax exemption number ⎕

Signature _____ Sales and use tax number _____

SHIP ORDER TO: (If other than above)

Name _____

Address _____

City/State/Zip _____

Telephone _____ Purchase Order (if required) _____

☐ Please ship back-ordered items as soon as possible

☐ Please cancel order for items out of stock   *(Catalog number 03145)*

☐ Please send _____ copies of *Haunted Inheritance* . . . at $5.95 each.

☐ Please send me the CompCare Catalog of more books and materials for growth-centered living. (No charge.)

PLEASE FILL IN BELOW FOR CHARGE ORDERS
Or enclose check for total amount of order.

Prices subject to change without notice.

Account No (12 or more digits) from your credit card

Check one
☐ VISA   ☐ MASTER CHARGE   Master Charge — also enter 4 digits below your account no

Your Card Issuing Bank _____
Expiration Date of Card _____
Credit Card Signature _____

TOTAL PRICE _____

4% Sales Tax _____
(Minnesota residents only)

Postage & Handling charge _____
Add 75 cents to orders totaling less than $15.00
Add 5% to orders totaling $15.00 or more

GRAND TOTAL _____
(U.S. dollars)

All orders shipped outside continental
U.S.A. will be billed actual shipping costs.

VISA®   **master charge**
THE INTERBANK CARD

CompCare® publications

A Division of the Comprehensive Care Corporation
Post Office Box 27777, Minneapolis, Minnesota 55427

for faster service on charge orders
call us toll free at:

800/328-3330

In Minnesota, call collect 612/559-4800

ORDER FORM

Date _____

| Order Number | Customer Number | Customer P.O. | ☐ ☐ ☐ ☐ ☐
1 2 3 4 5 | For Office Use Only |

| UPS 1 ☐ | PP 2 ☐ | PPD 3 ☐ | PPD CHGS 4 ☐ | WILL CALL 5 ☐ | OUR TRUCK 6 ☐ | CARRIER _____ |

BILL ORDER TO:

Name _____

Address _____

City/State/Zip _____

Non-profit organization, please show tax exemption number [_____]

Signature _____   Sales and use tax number _____

SHIP ORDER TO: (If other than above)

Name _____

Address _____

City/State/Zip _____

Telephone _____   Purchase Order (if required) _____

☐ Please ship back-ordered items as soon as possible

☐ Please cancel order for items out of stock

(Catalog number 03145)

☐ Please send _____ copies of *Haunted Inheritance* . . . at $5.95 each.

☐ Please send me the CompCare Catalog of more books and materials for growth-centered living. (No charge.)

PLEASE FILL IN BELOW FOR CHARGE ORDERS
Or enclose check for total amount of order.

Prices subject to change without notice.

Account No. (12 or more digits) from your credit card

[☐☐☐☐ ☐☐☐☐ ☐☐☐☐ ☐☐☐☐]   [☐☐☐☐]

Check one
☐ VISA   ☐ MASTER CHARGE   Master Charge — also enter 4 digits below your account no.

Your Card Issuing Bank _____

Expiration Date of Card _____

Credit Card Signature _____

TOTAL PRICE _____

4% Sales Tax _____
(Minnesota residents only)

Postage & Handling charge _____
Add 75 cents to orders totaling less than $15.00
Add 5% to orders totaling $15.00 or more

GRAND TOTAL _____
(U.S. dollars)

All orders shipped outside continental
U.S.A. will be billed actual shipping costs.

VISA®   **master charge**

PS
3555
.R623
H28
1980

6.95

PS
3555
.R623
H238

1980